WITHDRAWN

ALSO BY EUGENE LIM

Fog & Car

The Strangers

Dear Cyborgs

DEAR CYBORGS

Eugene Lim

FARRAR, STRAUS AND GIROUX   NEW YORK

Farrar, Straus and Giroux
18 West 18th Street, New York 10011

Copyright © 2017 by Eugene Lim
All rights reserved
Printed in the United States of America
First edition, 2017

Library of Congress Cataloging-in-Publication Data
Names: Lim, Eugene, author.
Title: Dear cyborgs : a novel / Eugene Lim.
Description: First edition. | New York : FSG Originals, 2017.
Identifiers: LCCN 2016045039 | ISBN 9780374537111 (softcover) |
    ISBN 9780374716417 (ebook)
Subjects: LCSH: Superheroes—Fiction. | Storytelling—Fiction. |
    BISAC: FICTION / Literary. | FICTION / Political. | GSAFD: Satire.
Classification: LCC PS3612.I46 D43 2017 | DDC 813/.6—dc23
LC record available at https://lccn.loc.gov/2016045039

Designed by Abby Kagan

Our books may be purchased in bulk for promotional, educational,
or business use. Please contact your local bookseller or the Macmillan
Corporate and Premium Sales Department at 1-800-221-7945, extension
5442, or by e-mail at MacmillanSpecialMarkets@macmillan.com.

www.fsgbooks.com • www.fsgoriginals.com
www.twitter.com/fsgbooks • www.facebook.com/fsgbooks

10 9 8 7 6 5 4 3 2

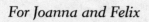

For Joanna and Felix

We are not machines!
—JEON TAE-IL

Catch me solving mysteries like Wikipedia Brown.
It's the future get down.
We make a sound even if nobody's around.
—DAS RACIST

Dear Cyborgs

Dear Cyborgs,

Today's puzzler. Enforced inescapable automatic insidious complicity. On the horizon no viable just alternative and no path toward one. All proposals thus far fanciful, impossible, doomed. Sure, optimism of the will. But—either from the towers or beyond the grid, in the trenches, amongst the ruins, or burb'd—what to do?

Yours mostly truly,

Origin Stories

This is in Ohio. We were eleven, twelve years old, and the teacher asked us to name the number of siblings we had. "One," most said, or, "Two." "Zero," a few said. I said, "One." Vu said, "Nine."

I burst out laughing because I'd been over to Vu's house a lot, had read comic books on his bed and kicked the soccer ball in his backyard, and had even eaten his mom's grilled cheese sandwiches. I'd never once seen the rustle of a brother-like or sister-like figment, ever, and so thought he was mocking the teacher. But Mrs. Clyde just moved on and no one added anything else, and Vu didn't make any adjustments to his claim.

When I asked him about this later, he just shrugged and said it was true, though he added, "Three are half." I didn't know how to pursue it and so let it drop and almost forgot about it entirely, except once in a while it would occur to me again and I would stop suddenly in the middle of something and say to myself, "Vu has nine invisible siblings." And I did this years and years later, long after Vu had died, and even then I'd find myself out of nowhere thinking, "Somewhere in the world are Vu's nine siblings, and I'll never know them."

(After doing it for some time, for years and decades, the habit of protest becomes something else, something apart from, almost irrelevant to, one's initial desires. It becomes, to say it simply, a way of life. Or, to be more accurate if less simple: one's initial ambitions regress into merely a way of living. Especially this is true if one is clever enough or lucky enough or cowardly enough—let's just say lucky . . . Especially when one is lucky enough not to have been crushed. And—this is the important qualifier—it must also be said that the methods of protest one has chosen, if one after a time is not crushed, that these methods of protest must have been entirely pathetic.)

I met Vu in a dream. Or rather I met him during a time of my life so separated from what happened before and later that I think of it as a dream. Most people must feel that childhood is that way, scenes that are familiar but irretrievable, a hazy dream—but I think those years in Ohio are for me a bit further removed than is typical. I'll try to explain.

My father was trained as an engineer, but he worked sporadically. He had a thin skin, was a binge drinker, and had a bad temper—a result of which was that he kept getting fired. And so the family kept moving. My memory of childhood therefore, *before* landing in that small town where I met Vu, is less a blur than a handful of orphaned film clips, too short and too few in number to add up to much. I remember only strange bits: the taste of dark chocolate in a neighbor's Oldsmobile, pink lotion on a girl's sunburn, a teacher's stare marked with hatred, a cut to my finger with my mother's razor. Bits with no story to them but my name.

And then at fifteen we moved again, to Chicago, and those small-town years got overwhelmed and momentarily erased by the seizures of adolescence and an immediate addiction to the convulsions of a city. And so, in this analysis, there is this bubble. An in-between time, eleven to fifteen, when I'm not quite a child and yet not an adult, where I now think, despite my feelings then of slow death through intricate paroxysms of boredom, I was nonetheless *safe*. And I knew I was safe, deep in my heart (perhaps crucially because I knew I didn't matter, because we were invisible, insignificant outsiders).

And my focus during this time of boyhood was Vu, whom I worshipped in a way I think not uncommon in boys of that age. I obsessed without acknowledging it but nonetheless with an open and even heady kind of love.

He introduced me to comic books. This, not incidentally, was also an introduction to sex and therefore adulthood, because we would gaze intensely at these idealized images, these cartoons of adult men and women in various forms of wish fulfillment or wish embroidering, in swift balletic action that echoed and manifested and were the seeds of our own desires.

Here is one lesson that Vu taught me. It maybe doesn't seem on the surface to be about comic books, but it is. At least if reading comic books was a sort of hedonistic, perhaps onanistic, act of defiance—and if one believes that such pursuits are coterminous with living. I'd gotten permission to spend the night at Vu's house. We would watch TV and read comic books and listen to music and talk. His mom ordered us a pizza but other than that we didn't see her. His father was never at home, and his mom kept to her room, so we had the run of their large and, from my point of view, deliciously shabby home. My own home, thanks to the rule of my father, in addition to the compulsions of my mother, was unforgiving in its order and cleanliness. It gleamed and was breathless and without beauty. So I first was shocked and then bewitched by the mess at the Nguyen home. (And shamefully misread its untidiness as entirely debauched, so once flung my pizza crust at the TV, which, to my confusion, appalled and enraged Vu.)

And in the mornings, when Vu woke up, instead of going directly to the bathroom or kitchen to do the various rituals required to begin the day, he would lazily pick through his comics and read one in bed. That was the revelation: that he could do this, that he was *allowed* to do it, that he had even conceived of it. It had, in other words, never occurred to me at the age of fourteen that the lounging, pajama-related activity one did in the evenings, after one's so-called homework and chores were done, could be done first thing in the morning, at the very start of the day, or really—and the extrapolation was immediately clear—one could do it whenever one wanted!

I was made suddenly to realize—Vu and his home taught this to me—that we were more animal than routine.

(However, there is a sliver of protest still possible, which you may rightfully accuse of being worse, a reactionary or collaborative tactic, but which nonetheless is a method I have come to subscribe to and furthermore think is the only possible defiance left outside of the terminal possibilities of suicide, the morally corrupting option of guerrilla warfare, or the subtly but fundamentally distinct choice of utter acquiescence. This alone-possible and admittedly vaporous defiance is merely to live and accept one's culpability but to try without going into heroics to participate minimally, as a parasite does, getting one's needs and not much more, not often much more. One tries then to touch only lightly the general degradation but also to become no longer concerned with it. One becomes accepting of powerlessness, is rendered complacent and mute, but tries nonetheless to signal to other like-minded parasites, not in order to gather and foment rebellion, which would be too grandiose a goal, but simply so as to provide reflection, the mirage or actuality of company, that is, simply to make known one's kind's existence as a remaining possibility. In the end this contemptible character I've sketched, the artist, is all that remains of the initial quest for purity.)

Later—and we discussed it only once, at night during a sleepover at my house, so perhaps we could allocate the confession to the subset of perhaps-a-dream—Vu told me a little more. In 1975, Vu's father, who was a respected scientist and who had ties to colleagues in the United States, was being persecuted by the Communists, and the entire family, in a moment of desperation and chaos and some subterfuge, had been airlifted out of Vietnam. It may have been true that Vu wasn't even his father's son but that of a killed relative. I don't think even Vu knew the entire story or the truth about his origins.

My parents were from South Korea. We were the only Asian boys in our grade (and except for Julie Chen, we were the only Asian kids in the entire county), and this fact, along with a few others, brought us together.

We bonded particularly over comic books, and our favorite was an "adult" title called *MunQu*, which the doughy proprietor of the mildewy comic-book store sold us with an attitude of acknowledged but silent conspiracy. It was less pornographic than "underground" in genre, meaning that what we delighted in, perhaps as much as the sighting of the occasional nipple, were its wise-ass swipes at Reagan (which we understood less as political satire than as savage pokes at our elders' puritanism and hypocrisy) and its seemingly mature take on recreational drug use. Its titular hero was a lanky, stoner chipmunk with bizarre martial arts skills coupled with troublesome anger management problems who mostly seemed to get into political squabbles with his unreasonably drawn girlfriend, a dark-haired skip tracer named Lana.

"Vu, you realize this's a bestiality book."

"Don't get your fingermits on it."

"Maybe more like mixed-race though."

"No poop, Perlock."

"You're saying its *enlightened* bestiality will make it worth something."

"Fool, my one through ten are bagged for a reason."

We were such outcasts that our isolation hardly pained us, as we could barely conceive of the alternative. We journeyed through junior high on an entirely separate path from the others. Almost everyone in this small town seemed to think this was for the best, but we did eventually find a group of others, those who had been shunned for their fatness or queerness or intelligence or non-Christian-ness, or some combination thereof—a familiar drama of Nerddom and xenophobia played out in small towns across the Midwest and South. The pariah status and bigotry seemed so inevitable and immutable a condition that we didn't think to complain—with one exception, for me, and that complaint had to do with girls. That—

privately, because I couldn't admit this even to Vu—was the one glaring glandular issue for which our ostracism did acquire a clear, sharp, gut-thrust injury, which seemed to have no cure and so left me cursing gods, crazed, horny, malevolent.

"Man, I can't wait to get out of this shithole," we both said, which, while true, was only one side of an eventually revealed paradox. Childhood was hell but also paradise. In retrospect it was safe because we had survived it. And so in it we were not yet destroyed or scarred or proven failures or dumb or worn-out or brokenhearted. And furthermore, the warmth of brotherhood never as cozy and pure as when the enemy surrounds, we *felt* happy while thinking we were suicidal. At least that was my case. Vu just got more and more angry.

In the winter about six months before my family moved to Chicago something changed at Vu's house, though I never fully understood what it was. I went over there one afternoon and discovered his home in even greater disarray than usual. Not abominable, but I did notice an extra layer of clutter and dirty dishes. At the same time the house seemed emptier. "Where's your mom?" I'd asked. "Out," he just said at first, but his mom never showed in the following days and eventually he admitted he was living alone.

"Where are they?"

"My dad took a job in L.A."

"And?"

"She went to help."

And that vague justification might have been the truth, but the fact was Vu lived alone, pretending at school that this was not the case, and telling only me.

I tried immediately not to remember this admission so I wouldn't feel guilty or have to think too hard on what it meant. And I was anyway distracted and excited because my father had recently announced we were going to move to Chicago at the end of the school year. Vu himself tried to shrug off his home situation, to make it seem a normal predicament, but even then I knew it bothered him. A fourteen-year-old boy is capable of taking care of himself, and what's more wants to believe he can, but no matter how he approached the situation, Vu knew he had been abandoned. He responded by hardening. If this is the right way to say it, Vu started to become around that time too comfortable with his own loneliness. Already a self-sufficient person, I saw him develop a haughtiness, an imperiousness that added another layer to his untouch-ability so that, for instance, even teachers seemed reluc-tant to engage or call on him.

In class, Vu was constantly doodling comic-book heroes. Simply by proximity, it seems, I began to follow suit, and though I was much less naturally talented, through hours and hours of practice I'd managed to become a decent drawer. We'd started making comics together, just strips

or sight gags, but also not a few minibooks of simple ad-
venture or sometimes wicked revenge fantasies. We never
really discussed them, just did them, on silent afternoons
or through the swapping of notebooks throughout the
school day.

In Ohio, drawing was useful mostly as a way to kill
time during those boring hours of invisibility. When I got
to Chicago I was surprised and delighted to find it actually had some social cachet, and through it I discovered a
group of friends. By the time high school was finishing I'd
even found a girlfriend, a half-Taiwanese girl who played
keyboards for a not-awful band. I drew all their concert
posters. By which I mean I drew three flyers for one afternoon performance at a coffeehouse.

And when I got to Chicago, almost in a superstitious
way, and also maybe in a cruel way that has to do with a
past love, I never tried again to get in touch with Vu.

Two days before we were to leave for Chicago, I spent
one last night at Vu's house. It was the very beginning of
summer vacation, and the week before, in the steamy last
days of school, Vu had taken me aside to tell me he'd
gotten us two tabs of acid. I wasn't surprised he could get
them—our town like many small towns was awash in
drugs—but I was surprised he wanted to try it. We hadn't
even smoked cigarettes, let alone pot, and we hadn't yet
tried to drink from the unopened boxes of Johnnie Walker
bottles I'd seen in his dad's office. Maybe the comics

could again be blamed. *MunQu* was penned, it was clear, by middle-aged hippies who often visited altered states and thought their access to these a natural right.

Taking drugs is a leap of faith—a secular, often doomed one: faith that it will be worth it, faith that you won't die, that it will all be okay—which is a leap I made out of love. Vu lived alone and even I was leaving him. Why not drop acid together?

I was on his floor looking at a Chris Claremont *X-Men.* He was reading something too, a Philip K. Dick novel called *Valis,* which he'd wanted me to read but that I hadn't gotten around to. My eyes were on the comic book, but I wasn't really looking at it because I knew he had the LSD and that we were going to take it. But, for some reason when I'd come over, instead of getting straight to it, we'd gone about our normal business, eating chips and reading comics and listening to music. Then, as if some internal clock had said it was time, Vu closed his book, rummaged through his backpack, and took out an envelope.

He handed me a blotter of the drug, a small piece of paper with a picture of Felix the Cat on it. We each put a tab on our tongue and then, wordlessly, went back to our reading. Two hours later we were lying down in his carpeted living room looking up and talking excitedly about the morphing animations the drug was creating out of his stucco popcorn ceiling. He saw frothy tsunamis while I was seeing running Ku Klux Klansmen—both illusions we took, fortunately, not only as benign but hilarious. A little after midnight we gorged on cold pizza and soda pop and by dawn we were coming down.

I was smiling when I left in the late morning, even though I was very sad to go. He smiled too. It had been a smart way to say goodbye. The next few days I was a mess. Hungover in a fragile way, I was tearful and quiet, which I was grateful my parents attributed, perhaps in a way correctly, to the trauma of the move.

Salt Star Thrower Flower

I'd gone back to the Zinc Bar, where I'd left the novel, but it was gone. Someone must have taken it. Annoyed, I stood outside the bar for several minutes weighing my options.

Should I walk to a bookstore, which may or may not have it, and pay full price for a replacement copy in order to support the store's enterprise, its development of community, and the habit of nonalgorithmic browsing? Or should I order it used online, where I could have it much cheaper and relatively quickly, but in doing so take part in the destruction of codex culture as well as most likely eliminating any chance of the author being meaningfully compensated? Or should I simply pirate a digital copy since the author was most likely getting no money anyway? Or, finally, should I just get it from a branch of the local public library?

I started walking aimlessly as this last option suddenly reminded me again of Ms. Mistleto.

After Bosnia-Herzegovina, the next time I saw her was

when the NSA was alerted that one of its data centers had been compromised. A server farm nestled in the bowels of Fort Meade had been breached. These computers held the phone and internet usage logs of all those citizens who were terrorist suspects as well as the phone and internet usage logs of all those citizens who were not terrorist suspects.

When the NSA director was at home masturbating to pornography, animated heads of Chelsea Manning and Edward Snowden appeared on his computer screen. The cartoon chorus of Manning and Snowden, who appeared as bobbleheads on the actors' bodies, said that I, Frank Exit, should retrieve the stolen files from their thief, Ms. Mistleto, by coming alone to meet her in the stacks of the Jaffna Public Library in Sri Lanka at midnight in three days' time.

And so in the next forty-eight hours a great many forces were marshaled. When I touched down at Bandaranaike International Airport, the military and secret police of at least three nations had been coordinated and had quietly surrounded the library with various personnel and equipment. However, that night, when I entered the library, alone per instructions, Ms. Mistleto wasn't there. Instead, as I stepped into a study hall, a projector powered on and a three-dimensional hologram of the masked Mistleto appeared. The hologram said, "I'm sorry I couldn't be here with you in the flesh, but I didn't want you to have an excuse to burn the place down while trying to capture me."

The holographic Mistleto then said:

One evening we heard, through a ripple of translations, Kim Jin-suk's words for the first time. She was at the top of a crane and on the other side of the world, and she spoke on a cell phone to a man who translated her words to a bystander, who in turn then yelled those words out to the crowd, who then in turn yelled those words farther out—a method of address dubbed the People's Microphone—and so ripples of phrases would eventually wash over us as we stood out at the edge of the crowd, figures who were hopeful yet passive. We heard:

> My friends who fight in Wall Street . . .
> in the heart of neoliberalism . . .
> This is Jin-suk Kim . . .
> Great to talk to you!

On October 6, 2011, we'd met and gone to Zuccotti Park after work to walk among the protesters and those others, like ourselves, who came to be near a moment that would exist only briefly, so that we could embody the flicker of their protest, a protest that seemed dangerous, that seemed real.

She was talking from crane number 85 of Hanjin Heavy Industries, in a shipyard in the port city of Busan, South Korea.

Eight years prior, in that same cramped control box at

the top of the crane, hovering a hundred and thirty feet in the air, in order to protest job losses, wage stagnation, arrests, intimidation by hired thugs, and the increasing persecution of workers, a man named Kim Joo-ik had hung himself after one hundred and twenty-nine days of similar occupying protest. He was a father of three, had worked in the shipyards since he was a teenager, and was a close friend to the woman who was there now.

Kim Jin-suk had chosen crane number 85 to honor her friend, and that evening to the milling crowd at Zuccotti Park she spoke careful words in deceptively easy and bright tones. She had already been living in that box in protest for nine months. We learned that she ate meals prepared by an initially small but then quickly growing number of supporters. These supporters used a pulley to bring up her food and change her waste bucket; they cheered her from beyond separating barricades and on Twitter. And eventually they came by the hopeful busload, a swelling movement that would number in the thousands. We learned that she had survived a freezing winter, monsoons, and then a summer sun that turned the metal box into an oven. And we learned that she was called *Salt Flower* after the pattern made from dried sweat on the overalls of the nation's workers. She said, "I went up without any thought of coming back down. I'd settled my affairs."

The crowd at Zuccotti Park cheered Kim Jin-suk's defiance and her words sent from across the globe, but then soon it moved on to other agenda topics, other speakers, other protests. Our attention drifted, and we soon found ourselves leaving the park.

(Later, for that entire winter when I visited the park repeatedly, and to an extent even now, these two became important images in my mind: the one a ragtag crowd crawling around a single city block, people drawn together by an impossible, almost invisible idea, and the other an inspiring but lonely self-exile swaying in her tiny prison high in the air.)

We went a few blocks away and found a Shanghainese restaurant one of us knew about. After we'd ordered and begun to eat, I turned to them and asked them what they thought, if they thought that it was all just hopeless, or if it was something. At first the others were quiet.

"I'm not sure," one of you said, finally. "It seems flimsy. Or childish. I guess childish, primarily. Like a spoiled kid having a tantrum. And equally powerless. It's annoying for the adults who have to respond, but they can't really take the tantrum very seriously."

I nodded once.

"What you say seems true," another said, "but on the other hand the protest also seems important. What's happening, what they're trying to do, seems to me vital."

"Yes, I agree one hundred percent," you said. "It *is* important. But let me ask you another question."

We nodded.

"We all agree what's happening is important, but what is it? What does it mean?"

There was a silence, but after a moment I said, "I'm not sure." Then, speaking slowly, I said, "I think it's in part an expression of hope and in part an expression of guilt." I paused again as I tried to articulate what had been circling through my mind these past weeks. "I guess, to put it another way, I think it's in part magical thinking and in part buyer's remorse."

"What do you mean?"

"I mean it's like the regret that comes after the purchase of something you don't really need and which isn't after all what you'd wanted. It's asking people to wake up to the fact that their desires have been manufactured, that the lives they are leading are modeled after flawed received ideas."

"Buyer's remorse. I think I see."

"As well, hidden in this remorse is another guilt, a knowledge that the entire social contract is contaminated, tainted, since it requires the hard labor of the unfortunate, as well as a violence to the earth and, importantly and even more subtly, an embedded faith in the eventual good of selfishness and greed. And this latter faith contains such an inherent conflict that at the minimum it creates a dangerous nerve damage, a desensitization, and at maximum necessitates either an idiocy or a self-hate."

"That's a little more complicated. But I guess what you're saying is it boils down to culpability. Is that right? A feeling of complicity to injustice."

"Yes, I think so."

"As well, there's the anger of those who have never

been able to buy at all," you added, and we nodded compulsorily.

"And the magical thinking?"

"This is an idealism, a hope. As when someone is dead and you pray for them to be alive again. Which is an impossibility and yet one still has that dream. To escape the current state, which seems, despite what I've just said about remorse, a stable and perfect and *permanent* projection of our selfish natures . . . To escape this, well, to escape this is like willing the dead back to life. It's an impossible wish, yet deeply human, a desire to transcend our limitations. That's why it's important. It expresses an impossible desire as if it were not impossible." I stopped before saying the next bit because I was less sure of it. "And I guess the crux of the matter is whether this expression of the impossible can somehow lead to its possibility, that is, to it no longer being impossible."

The one who'd asked the question nodded thoughtfully and then said, "For the most part I agree with what you're saying, but there's another, more cynical interpretation."

"What is that?"

"That this is indeed an 'expression of the impossible,' just like you say. But the reason it's important is because that's all it will ever be. Wishful thinking. And rather than a site or spark for the beginning of the impossible made possible, it's just a way for excess and agitating energies to play themselves out, for these to be released in a harmless and managed way. There is almost a natural engineering—not a conspiracy but simply an organic process—where a necessary and temporary aggregation of revolutionary forces occurs in order to bring about their elimination, either by actual destruction or, more effectively, by their co-optation into a toothless brand. Or, if absolutely necessary, after great effort and loss, cosmetic or otherwise deceptive reforms will be enacted—but these usually just better camouflage for an otherwise unchanged apparatus."

We fell then into another silence, sipping our cold tea. Eventually the one who had mostly been listening, who had mostly been quiet until now, took the lid of the teapot in front of us and flipped it over. Shortly after, a fresh pot was brought out. She poured for us and then lifted her cup but held it in front of her mouth with two hands, elbows on the table and looking pensive. She said, "Loren Eiseley's language is considered a little old-fashioned today but it's so in a way I love. 'The Star Thrower' is one of his better-known essays, and it's a tale one could probably negate as wishful thinking. It concerns a man in an even worse position than all of you." She said this to us with a little smile.

"A despairing man," she continued, "is having a spiritual crisis that has nearly crushed him. On a beach this deeply troubled fellow comes across someone throwing dying starfish back into the ocean. These dying animals are numberless on the beach, and in fact it's become a kind of sport with the tourists to collect the strewn sea life, which are considered a delicacy, and cook them. In contrast to these, the Star Thrower spends his time saving starfish by throwing them back into the ocean one at a time. And he does this despite the surf's continuous and insurmountable holocaust. In the Star Thrower—in this figure of impossible ambition—the despairing man finds hope and redemption.

"You can call it just a bromide if you wish," she went on. "And in fact there's a sort of debased, more sentimental version of this story that motivational speakers use where the Star Thrower, who sometimes is a little girl, sometimes a Christ-like figure if not Christ himself, is asked why she does what she does, what difference it could possibly make. And she responds simply, after twirling another starfish back into the ocean, 'It made a difference for that one.'

"So I think that a protest," she went on, "like a work of dance or a work of music, is something done, at least in part, by the protester *for* the protester."

She saw I was about to interrupt so said, "One more minute. Let me explain. Of course one hopes and plans for impact, for audience, for change, for efficacy. But, like dance, like music, a protest can be a religious ritual too, one that needn't be derisively looked down upon as magical thinking, but a spiritual act where the act itself is the goal. And that act may on some other level be co-opted, but in the subjective world of the protester it is a way, in itself, to be. Even in solipsism, the subject can be moral. You can call it hokum if you wish, but for the protester, the protest makes a moral world in which she can abide."

The holograph of Ms. Mistleto flickered and then winked out of existence. In the quiet of the Jaffna Public Library, I all at once found myself in the dark and alone.

Origin Stories

"Dear Cyborgs,"

When looking for something to save my place in the novel I was reading, I thought once again about how I might close the gap that had grown between myself and my sister, who now seemed so much a stranger to me. The novel was coming to its conclusion, and while it was intriguing, I was disappointed and thought of it only as an instrument to pass the time. Nonetheless I wanted to know what happened to the main character, a detective, and so, despite being late for lunch with my friend Muriel, took a minute to dig around for a bookmark so I could more easily resume the story later that night, or perhaps the next day, when I had more time.

On my desk I managed to find a postcard someone had sent to me, Frank Exit. "Dear Cyborgs," it started on one side. On the other it had a photograph of a minaret, which a caption told me was from the Umayyad Mosque of Aleppo. After the salutation, I read, "Ms. Mistleto is your sister." It was unsigned. In my profession I tended to get a lot of crank letters.

I slipped the postcard into my novel and then, as if struck by some urgency (but what could it be?), began rushing, putting on my socks and shoes in a kind of fury. I wasn't sure why I suddenly was so anxious about being just a few minutes late (and why only moments before I had been leisurely flipping through papers on my desk in search of a good bookmark), but now I cursed (goddamn shoelaces!) as I fumbled with my sneakers and slammed the door to my fourth-floor walk-up and bounded down the stairs two at a time. I set off at a brisk pace. I actually wasn't far from the restaurant where I'd agreed to meet my friend, only a twenty-minute walk, even less if I hurried.

When I got to the restaurant Muriel was already there and had gotten us a table. The restaurant was an airy and polished place, one I'd never really taken to, except that while it mostly served unremarkable Thai food in asymmetrical dishware, it also featured a very affordable lunch special and a decent iced tea. Muriel and I (she lived just a few blocks from the restaurant, that helped too) therefore often wound up here for lunch. When I'd entered I'd been momentarily surprised to see that she had brought our friend Dave, but didn't mind at all, as I found Dave an amusing presence, very polite and thoughtful in a way I admire. We hadn't known Dave for very long but had had recently some shared adventures (and I also had the suspicion that Muriel was interested in him romantically).

As soon as I sat down, the waitress came to take our order. After she'd done this and just before leaving our table she collected our menus and said something I couldn't understand exactly, but it seemed to me she whispered (with a smile), "I'm not doing this for you. I'm doing this for me." And then she turned and we watched her leave.

Then Dave said, "For some time I'd been working on these drawings. At first they started out as one thing, and then they turned into something else, and then they turned closer to that first thing—but now with extra knowledge, if you know what I mean.

"It's often like that," he continued, "and I think the best work is when you don't have a plan, just a few rules. Not that I'm against grand architecture or ambitious engineering. Or maybe I am. It's just like anything else, I guess. You have to have a sense of balance.

"Many years ago a friend gave me an expensive set of colored pencils. I'd made some drawings with them at the time but then put them away, always thinking I'd use them later. But I never did.

"She killed herself last year, my friend, the one who'd given me the pencils.

"I hadn't seen her recently. Last I'd heard, she'd moved to Albuquerque and then to Portland, Oregon.

"But around when we'd first met she'd given me this

refined, very delicate set of colored pencils. I was impressed and happy, but then after making just a few drawings, I put them away and didn't think about them until years later.

"I'd met her at a party I'd gone to outside of Brattle-boro. Her name was Ursula. Some rich gallerist was having a weekend-long party and somehow I'd been invited. This was when Ursula and I were both in our twenties. The party was held in the early summer at this rich person's estate, which was quite beautiful and impressive, with sprawling grounds containing green hills that backed into a dense wood.

"Ursula was Bangladeshi and we happened to be the only nonwhite people at the party. That was probably how the conversation started. Some snarky, self-defending remark—and the other chimed in and laughed.

"We got along well and took a few walks around the grounds together. Nothing romantic ever happened, though I would not have at all minded if it had. There was something important about those conversations, a recognition of a particular excitement that it was crucial to acknowledge but a recognition that needed to be done slyly. In any case, we made promises to see each other back in the city—promises each probably was surprised that the other kept.

"I didn't realize it at the time, but Ursula was already quite a successful artist. She was being collected and shown. Her work straddled the line between sculpture and painting, and—since she was a woman—people made easy comparisons between her and Elizabeth Murray or

Lee Bontecou or Eva Hesse, but really she was nothing like any of these. Her process was very physical, a wrestling or slow-dancing with the materials at a glacial beat. This was subverted by her palette, which was candy-colored and light: pastels and neons. The work was immediately identifiable, which is almost all that is required in our current marketplace to be richly compensated and then quickly desaturated by co-optation.

"But she came up with a kind of defense. One day she made a painting called *Ursula's Curse*, which consisted of just a few sentences in white block lettering against a black background. It read:

> This painting cannot be bought or sold for more than the total wages of six months full-time employment at the minimum wage as determined by the state of New York. If this painting should be sold for greater than this amount, may both the buyer and seller be considered shit by the entire world and by themselves, and may they spend the afterlife as sad and angry and hungry and hopeless as poverty makes.

"It caused a small sensation. She put her curse on the back of all her works from then on. Others followed suit. For a time it was in vogue, and it seemed at least a tonic or a limit to the art market's baseness had been found.

"But then people began criticizing her number, saying, why six months? And why New York? They said it was a naïve understanding of capital or that it was just another bourgeois stunt, or a well-intentioned but flawed gesture. And then the gallerists and critics just began quietly to not return her calls, to shun her. It was insidious, a subtle process—but within a year she was dropped from her gallery, went unmentioned in reviews, and was completely marginalized. The money, in other words, responded to her threat with its immense, stealthy powers.

"Then the difficulties really began." Dave paused and took a few sips of tea. "She had been working with an industrial putty she'd discovered. She'd found she could make enormous sculptural reliefs with it. She would mold and work the putty and then drive it to a factory on Long Island and bake it in huge ovens where it took on a deep amethyst hue.

"It was satisfying work. But each night her hands hurt more and more. At first it was a pleasant kind of ache, an organic feedback, a kind of silent and karmic applause—or so she said she thought it. But then the pain grew worse, until, eventually, it became unbearable and she was forced to abandon the work. She thought she could just rest, take a break or try another medium, but the pain wouldn't go away.

"It turned out to be an aggressive form of arthritis. The disease grew worse and in only a few years she could barely hold a pen or type. She had to give up art-making completely. Her hands became twisted, permanently deformed.

"I didn't see her much after that. She started traveling, looking for a cure or some kind of treatment, going to

Norway and China and then living for a time on the West Coast. We lost touch. When I learned last winter that she'd taken her life, I realized we hadn't spoken in several years.

"Even though they'd ignored her for so long, after her suicide the art critics responded with their usual self-serving nostalgia. Her commercial protest was reframed as a now historical (and therefore toothless) but valiant defiance. Mutual friends began writing little memorials and asked me to do the same. I refused, which angered them, but I couldn't understand this need to ingratiate oneself before the dead, especially by lying, which is all one ever does.

"And yet again she was constantly in my thoughts. By then I was working at the advertising firm, and so in be-tween fiddling with some bus poster for a bank or a web animation for a new brand of soda, my thoughts would turn to her.

"And after a while, almost unthinkingly, I pulled out the box of colored pencils she had given me that summer when we'd first met, during a time in my life when I had expected everything was going to turn out so different.

"Not quite thinking of her but not quite not thinking of her, I began drawing with them.

"I started drawing landscapes at first—bucolic scenes: fields and hills and streams. Right away I thought they were turning out well, almost like something was guiding my hand. But they were also a little sentimental. At first I thought they were just dream pictures, just images of unreal places—but slowly I realized I was drawing scenes from that weekend party in Vermont. Almost as soon as I realized this, the drawings started getting worse, as if in my coming to understand what I was trying to tell myself, the crucial energy had dissipated.

"I tried to respond by enhancing the core weakness, by making them even more sentimental, making them more consciously about an early summer and about being with other young people and about living a waking dream about future, unlived lives. But they kept taking on an irony I didn't intend. I had wanted to maintain that feeling of yearning and expectation.

"But the drawings kept getting worse and worse.

"And then one day I stopped drawing the landscapes and started making abstract pictures.

"I don't know why I changed, and it was more natural, a slipping away and into, than any conscious decision.

"These new drawings immediately were denser, full of scribbles and layers. Something told me I was also drawing landscapes but of a different kind. And shortly later still I realized I was trying to sketch the place Ursula had gone to, or, maybe more accurately, the place she had become. So that *Where's Ursula?* was the absolute title of these works in my mind.

"And whereas before I'd found that the pictures had gotten worse at precisely the moment I'd come to consciously understand what I was doing, *now*, by acknowledging the question—maybe since it *was* a question—the drawings became better, deeper and more ponderous and richer.

"I also concluded that if anyone else ever saw these drawings, in order for them to really see them, I could never tell them the name I'd given the drawings, for this would direct them in too simple and immediate a way.

"And yet since I couldn't conceivably show these drawings without acknowledging their debt to Ursula, I knew I was in a bind and could never really show them to anyone. I knew there would be no way for anyone to truly see them as they actually were. I didn't mind but thought it was an interesting trap I'd placed myself in.

"After a few months of this I stopped sketching once again.

"I didn't draw for quite a while after that. I was, during that time, still thinking of Ursula and still being pulled back to her pencils, but I wasn't quite ready to draw again, not yet. I was working out something in the back of my mind. I knew I had to be patient.

"And then one day I saw on a television show, just in a quick transition scene, a truck painting a dashed yellow line down the middle of a highway. Suddenly I knew what I was going to do, and I went to a supply store and bought long rolls of white paper.

"I began to create a routine for myself.

"Every day after dinner I'd take out one of Ursula's pencils, and I'd start coloring in a section of paper. My goal was to color in the paper as completely as possible. I was trying to use up the pencil entirely, down to its last nub. I would work until I couldn't hold it properly anymore and was rubbing the paper with the very tips of my fingers.

"When I was done each night the sun would be long gone and my fingers would be cramped and my hand would throb and I thought of what Ursula had said about a silent, karmic applause.

"After a month of this practice the pencils were gone. And I was left with several scrolls of the now-colored paper.

"Then one day just last week I decided to burn the colored scrolls.

"And I burned also the abstractions I'd privately titled *Where's Ursula?*

"And I burned also the drawings of that summer weekend in Vermont.

"And that was that," Dave said.

It was quiet for a few moments. I wanted to say something to lighten the mood, to make a joke and so relieve him and us, but there seemed no way to do it, and the sad silence lingered on for some time.

But then Muriel said, almost out of nervousness, "I know *exactly* what you mean. *Exactly.* I had the same feeling when I was young, sixteen, to be precise. At sixteen I was a precocious girl—ugly, too.

"My ugliness," she continued, "if ugliness is a description of the reaction of others, came to torture me and aggravated my adolescent fury nearly to the point of self-annihilation. My parents were at their wits' end and, in an act of desperation, thinking crazy might be the medicine for crazy, arranged for me to take art lessons with a Pilipino artist named Frederick Moreno, an obvious alcoholic, a vague colleague of my mother's at the university, a mediocre painter but very gifted raconteur and survivor of our city's catty art biome.

"Moreno," Muriel went on, "let me take up space in his studio. Every day he would work on his blue-and-gray geometric paintings (utterly boring, I'd thought even then), perched on a stool with his back toward the window, a position that took advantage of the light but did not offer the distraction of a view—which happened to be splendid, looking down a wide and lively avenue—listening to the classical music station at low volume, humming and handsome, with a heavy glass tumbler whose contents glowed amber in the after-school light. I chose to sit in the room's opposite corner sketching dark and crude portraits, at first of him or my parents or classmates, teachers, other enemies. Every so often he'd come by and say a word or two. Nothing particularly instructive. A generic or weak encouragement: 'Good job' or 'Keep at it.'

"But then slowly, over the next few months, he grew increasingly interested in what I was working on. He wouldn't say so, but he would come and look more and more frequently and his questions seemed more and more pointed. But I didn't care about him. I'd discovered something far more important. Those afternoons (temporarily,

I would discover) had unlocked a door. Simply, I had had an idea, a vision, of what I could create.

"One day a few months later I finished a painting, and I knew this latest series was done, and that a vision had been made manifest. It was an uncanny sort of satisfaction. I wasn't necessarily sure the paintings would be interesting to others, but I knew I had captured in them something complex and savage from within. And also I knew that this act of capture or exorcism, calmly worked up to but with a hidden trepidation—a carefully sidestepped but titanic fear of disappointment—had brought with its final achievement a strange and hollow peace.

"That night, at two or three in the morning, I went to the kitchen and found the tea tin where my parents kept their marijuana. I'd never smoked but had watched them many times. I rolled an imperfect but passable joint and went out for a walk. It was a cool spring night, and I'd only worn a T-shirt. I found myself shivering but wasn't uncomfortable. I made my way to a bridge that floated several stories above a wide black canal. For years the water in this canal had been extremely polluted and had once, embarrassingly, even caught fire. That night the water was a black oily mirror reflecting a cold moon and the outline of the bridge and of the nearby buildings. I thought it was perfect and sat looking down at the reflection while every so often taking long, contemplative tokes on my improvised cigarette. I stood up and made ready to jump.

"It wasn't clear the leap would be fatal. I could die or

I could be maimed or I could survive. It seemed a test, not for myself but for the cosmos. My body—broken, intact, or a corpse—would be the mark, the grade, by which the universe would be judged. That was my school-girl thought.

"I blacked out. I must have jumped but I don't re-member doing so, though often since that night I've lain in bed and indulged in a dream of the tumble. I reimag-ine it since I don't remember it. A confusion of black sky with black water, stars and moon and buildings and clouds spinning in the air. Cold air and then colder water. Death and life.

"I broke my back but miraculously survived. Some-one saw my jump, the one I can't remember, and called the police and thereby saved my life. This anonymous witness says I hit a pylon on my drop, the consequence of which is that I still walk with a slight limp, luckily the extent of any permanent damage.

"I spent several months in the hospital, enjoying the nearness to death and illness but disgusted by the con-stant protocols for hygiene and the smells of disinfec-tant and rubber, which for some reason I found artificial, vaguely sacrilegious, and hypocritical. I was still some-what under the influence of my vision.

"When I was about to be released I was surprised by a visit from Moreno.

"He told me he had worked on a gift for me. He said that the following week I should pay a visit to an address he gave me. I asked my parents about it but they wouldn't reveal what was going on. They would only say they'd given Moreno their permission. I wasn't really in the mood for surprises but curiosity got the better of me, and so the following week I took a cab by myself to the downtown address Moreno had scribbled down.

"It turned out to be a gallery. I stepped through the wide polished doors into rooms that smelled of sawdust and drywall and through which floated also, like a delicate perfume, the unmistakable odor of wealth. I walked inside to see my paintings hanging on the walls, justifying themselves in that obscene way—or so said the fever inside me at the time, which still hadn't broken and which visits me some days still—and I felt a surge of bile clench my stomach and make ready to surge in fitful pumps up my throat. I spun around, walked outside, and puked on the sidewalk. I then immediately went back home, packed a bag, wrote a note, stole five hundred dollars, and left town."

I'd heard Muriel's story before, many times, in fact, and it was clear to me that she'd told her tale as some kind of preliminary mating ritual, a flirting gambit for Dave's benefit, so there was no way I was going to interrupt her (though I did wonder if the tactic wouldn't scare Dave and therefore backfire). However, I also was eagerly looking for an opportunity to talk about my estranged sister. She had abandoned her family, and last I'd heard, she was living alone in a run-down apartment on the other side of town. All this was still on my mind and something I wanted to get my friends' opinion on.

But after Muriel was done talking, suddenly I thought that Dave, who hadn't yet heard about *my* past, might be interested in hearing about it, so I said to my friends, "Yes, I agree entirely. *Entirely.* I mean, I know exactly what you're both saying. For me, I come at it from a different perspective, of course. But nonetheless.

"I was a writer," I continued. "Maybe I still am. I don't know. Sometimes I still try, but I've a bad case of block.

"What happened was about a decade ago I published a collection of stories. These were old-fashioned moral tales disguised as science fiction. The stories revolved around the affairs of young technocrats who discovered that the mechanized times they'd created had, alas, made them, without their consent, no longer human.

"Back then I thought my stories were brave and maybe even visionary. Now I think they're heavy-handed and a bit riskless.

"But for whatever cyclical and lucky reason, the book was a minor hit. I saw it displayed flush out in all the better bookshops, it had decent sales, and I was given a contract and advance for a novel that I outlined to my agent and publisher in purposefully vague terms.

"I went through that advance very quickly and without having made any progress on the proposed novel. Even though I was trying daily to deliver what I'd promised,

I couldn't bring myself to do it. It wasn't writer's block then, not exactly. At the time I knew what was expected.

"What was expected was a slightly modified coming-of-age novel that traded on my Korean-American identity. Something not too obviously an assimilation tale—and above all clever—yet also something not too much a deviation from that sellable idea, so that the marketplace of culture could easily absorb my story without being too discomfited. Even if no one had said this aloud, to me it was clear as day that this was the assignment.

"And I was willing to do it! It wasn't ethics that seemed to make the job impossible, but rather, I think, an underdeveloped sense of humor. I couldn't laugh it off. I couldn't get in the right mood. To sell that subject, which, to overgeneralize, is one step past the melodrama and pathos of the first generation's suffering. That is, in order to sell the second generation's schizophrenia and double-agenthood, one needs to pepper the thing with jokes, so you can say, See, I'm no victim, not only. I'm in on it, am injured by living in two worlds but yet whole and not broken, in fact, fortified and special in my elasticity, in the ability to be both of and other. *That* took a certain comic ability I discovered I did not have.

"Many months went by and I'd delivered nothing, but then my agent called me with an offer. She knew the novel wasn't coming along and that I was hurting for money. A certain Chinese-American politician, really ex-politician due to a recent scandal, needed a ghostwriter to help him with his autobiography, which he hoped would help rehabilitate him or at least firm up his legacy. Even though I was untested and frankly not a little naïve, simply because we were both Asian American, even though it made no sense, people thought to put us together.

"He had been a city council member and a two-time mayoral candidate before a fund-raising scandal brought him down. He needed something different, therefore, to allow him to rise from the political ashes, something more than just the usual inspirational pap. If he'd wanted the usual, all he had to do was fill out the bio he stumped with and which got reproduced with prominent placement on his ineffectual campaign pamphlets.

"No, he told me when I met him—before a series of marathon interviews—he needed something much more poetic and complicated. He needed a biography that detailed darker subplots in his life—perhaps odd sexual-awakening or drug-abuse stories, perhaps lessons from having to bear witness to financial misconduct—who knew what exactly, that was for me to figure out. But whatever I came up with, it had to be placed somehow in the reader's mind that these experiences, from which this man must have the appearance of having emerged if not unscathed then at least uncorrupted, had also imprinted upon him the worldly wisdom that would give him the insight to make just the right compromises when amid the deafening roar and blinding whiz of the legislative machine's incomprehensible moving bits.

"It was an impossible job: to make a lyric (and relatable) poetry out of the mundane shortcomings of a commonly ambitious man. I signed up immediately.

"All of a sudden the globby lump of inability I'd confronted for the better half of the previous year, a time spent trying to strategically fictionalize my identity, began quivering with potential. Practically before my eyes I began to witness a startling alchemy. I saw this piece of constipated shit—the themes and events of my short life— transmuted into a golden narrative that I channeled into a roller-coaster picaresque of eventual triumph from darker forces, something that came to be gloriously subtitled: *The Jack Hu Story.*

"I was ecstatic. The anonymity of the ghostwriting contract gave me permission to use all the underhanded emotionally manipulative tricks I couldn't have borne to see enter the world under my own name. But knowing that these would merely appear as a higher-end version of hackwork, what harm, I thought, could it do to myself or others?

"I labored hard, through weeks of punishing all-nighters and a month of rewrites. On the other hand I discovered how untortured writing could be when telling other people's lies.

"Two seasons later I saw my efforts introduced into the world in hardcover, with an embossed and impeccably designed dust jacket, my name of course nowhere found in this glossy and heavily marketed product. And then a mere few election cycles later, the man, now a senator, I was touched, robocalled me late at night to remind me as *one of his staunchest supporters* to get out the vote."

I thought I'd spun a funny tale, but Muriel's stink-eye informed me I'd overdone it and that my cynical tone was tactless, that I was a killjoy and perhaps insensitive somehow to Dave's grief. I was about to apologize or somehow backpedal, but I didn't get a chance, because just as I was about to speak, the commissioner's alarm vibrated in my pocket.

I looked at my friends and knew that they had just received the same signal, so we quietly and quickly paid our bill and left. Together Muriel and I form a secret vigilante superhero group called Team Chaos. Even though she works as a social worker and even though she'd rather be a poet and a painter, Muriel is actually a foundling extraterrestrial sent from a far superior civilization. She can fly, walk through walls, and shoot powerful beams from the palms of her hands. This origin and her superpowers were revealed to her only on her thirty-fifth birthday (a shock, as you might imagine). I'm a mere Earthling and therefore far less inherently powerful, but I've mastered various physical disciplines and martial arts as well as having proven myself in battle with a certain tactical wiliness, which seems to impress. Despite these accomplishments, as you no doubt will notice, I tend to be depressed and anxious much of the time. Dave has recently joined Muriel and me on a few adventures, including stopping Boss Mighty's mind-control scheme and helping inoculate the planet against the deadly Xfoolinghi space disease. He is *very* good with a slingshot.

In no time at all we were in our secret-identity costumes and had arrived at the police commissioner's underground bunker. He came in at a brisk pace and waved his hands, saying, "I'm very sorry, Team Chaos. It was a misunderstanding. It looked like a wormhole was going to open up and send a massive surge of Garno-plasma directly at our city, but it turned out to just be a software glitch. I hope I didn't disrupt your day too much."

"No problem," said Dave, who is always so affable in these types of situations. "We had just been talking over lunch."

"Good, good," said the commissioner, "but my apologies again." He then paused and said, "Well, since you're all here, can I ask your advice on something?"

We all went pretty far back with the commissioner, so I said, "Sure thing, Ira. What's on your mind?"

"It's all this new technology," he began. "It's really taking a toll on my ability to concentrate. Every time I want to go sit and read a novel or even listen to some music, I can only do so for a few minutes before I get distracted. Even when I watch a movie at home I'm constantly looking things up, the names of actors or other movies or just trivial facts. And I really worry about my children, who are growing up with these constant distractions, and who seem to have never really known any habit of extended concentration at all."

Muriel, Dave, and I then took turns comforting the commissioner with all the regular platitudes and told him everything would be okay, that we were an adaptable race, and that the kids would no doubt be all right. But deep down we, too, were worried about the future. We left the commissioner's underground bunker a little cranky, as is common when taking up a position one doesn't really believe in.

Dave suggested we go home and meet at the karaoke bar later that night.

"Okay," I said. I bid farewell to my friends and then decided to take advantage of the pleasant weather to walk home.

Dear Cyborgs,

Today's puzzler. The always abiding indeterminacy.
The fog of war. Externalities. Unintended
consequences compounding. You are an agent in the
storm and the moment for hand wringing is over. So,
what will it be: French fries? Or the salad?

Yours semi-truly,

Ghost ın the Assembly

When I got back to my apartment I was tired, and thought I'd just sit and have a glass of cold water and read my detective novel. I went to my desk where I thought I'd left it, but it wasn't there. When I was in a rush to put on my shoes and meet Muriel I must have flung it someplace.

I looked around and went back and forth looking for the book in the exact same places several times, thinking, I guess, that the book might reappear if I blinked. But it wasn't the case. And after I'd gone over the same path four times, I realized I was too distracted and tired to search any further. It was a shame, as there was nothing I wanted more than to escape into the thrill of Inspector Mush Tate's hunt for her chief foil, the evil but seductive, exhibitionistic yet mysterious Boss S. Car.

The loss of my book, which I hoped was momentary, made me think I wanted a different kind of beverage. When I'm reading I like to keep a clear, crisp mind. I don't like then to drink alcohol, and even coffee or tea can make me overexcited. But *since I can't find the book,*

I thought with a sigh, *there really isn't anything else to do.* So I poured myself a tequila and sat on the couch. Over the course of half an hour our part of the earth shifted away from the sun, changing the sky's colors, and I sat watching this transformation in silence.

While the room was filling with dark purple shadows, for one reason or another I began recalling a long and cold day and night I'd lived through about fifteen years prior. It had to do with the kidnapped children of a Japanese diplomat.

There were some sensitive trade negotiations going on with Japan at the time (some kind of power brokering about which I was never entirely informed), and because of this and because of the revealed methodology of the kidnapper, I was tapped for the job.

The terrorist group that had claimed responsibility for the kidnapping was led by someone who called herself Ms. Mistleto. Little was known about her other than her name.

The Japanese diplomat's children had gotten on a plane in Tokyo that was destined for Paris. They were on their way to spend two weeks at a tennis camp in Monaco. The flight had had one transfer in Doha, Qatar. The children were traveling with their tutor-cum-bodyguard, a very capable man I interviewed named Humbert. Humbert was found drugged and unconscious in a bathroom stall in a railway station in Omsk, Siberia. He recalls getting on the plane in Tokyo and nothing else until he awoke in a hospital thirty-six hours later.

Two days after the kidnapping, a letter oddly addressed to Ira—my friend, the police commissioner—was sent to the Japanese embassy in Berlin. Ira, to his knowledge, had never had anything to do with the Japanese economy or international politics, so it was assumed the gesture and the contents of the letter were for my benefit. I'd been on my vigilante crime-fighting crusade for several years by then and, despite a desire and need for anonymity, my reputation had become well known. In fact, I had attracted some very unwanted attention. In these circles of which I'm speaking I was known by the alias Frank Exit.

The ransom letter had several demands: the adoption worldwide of a single-payer universal health care system, mandatory carbon caps, nuclear disarmament, paid yearlong parental leave, and a tax on all securities transactions. "Ms. Mistleto," the signer of the ransom note, thoughtfully added that since such demands would not be easily met, she would accept in the meantime, as a down payment and a token of good faith, so-called, the artist Robert Rauschenberg's *Canyon*—a sculptural combine deemed priceless by some assessors (but tagged at $65 million by the Internal Revenue Service)—delivered to a given set of GPS coordinates in a week's time. The sculpture needed to be delivered by someone unarmed and alone. Which is how I got involved; I was to be the courier.

The coordinates for the ransom delivery happened to be a remote and barely accessible point three quarters up one of the lesser peaks of the Himalayan range. A thin, snow-covered, barely marked track led up this mountain, and I was supposed to drag the combine behind me in a special sledge provided expressly for that purpose. I'd find it at a kind of base camp at the foot of the mountain, where there would also be the only other equipment and attire I was allowed for the ascent.

Even the shirt on my back was predetermined. All of this severely restricted my options, as I had, in my vigilantism, depended often on military-grade high technology to trick or outflank or outgun or otherwise defeat my various uncanny foes. On this trip I was required to confront my opponents with none of my regular armaments; in fact, I felt I'd be meeting them naked and as vulnerable as a newborn.

Furthermore, I discovered when I arrived at the designated base camp a few days later—alone but with a clever forgery of the Rauschenberg sculpture—the clothing I found there was nearly inadequate for the journey. Threadbare shirts, broken boots, thin gloves, a mangy wool sweater, and a greatcoat with holes. I grimaced as I took off my impact- and cut-resistant self-heating nano-neofleece-lined gloves and put on their crude cotton ancestors. I similarly took off my quad-layered tech-down parka with its ripstop nylon shell, and the rest of my carefully chosen gear, and put on Ms. Mistleto's provided hand-me-downs.

I was shaking even before I left the little hut, but doubled over in pain when I stepped outside. The icy wind slammed into me as if I'd run full-speed into a wall, and I felt exhausted after only a few steps.

Fortunately, the sledge carrying the sculpture seemed of passable quality. I estimated it would take ten hours to reach the drop-off site, and I wondered and then fought off wondering if I would live to see the next day.

After three hours of trudging through the snow with the oxygen deprivation of the altitude, which gave me a crushing headache just fractionally less debilitating than a grand mal seizure, I began to suffer terrifying hallucinations of falling icy boulders and drooling clawed giants with the visage of our fortieth president. It seemed every tenth step had me falling through a drift up to my thigh, having lost and then found and then lost and then found the blurry trail several times. I was in a constant panic and, though the sun was out and it was clear, I was growing despairingly assured I would lose my toes and fingers to frostbite.

I dreamed of karaoke bars and tequila. There were sorrowful moments when I contemplated women I'd loved. I was saddened by how easily I'd forgotten the hours and days and months spent in their company. I thought of the houses I'd lived in as a child and beds in which I'd been sick. I had nightmares of violent hand-to-hand battles with crime kingpins and brilliant anarchic psychopaths, each strengthened by insatiable greed or hate-inflamed anger or, worse, berserker insanity. And I relived battles where instead of making the perfect calculation at precisely the right time, I was too slow or too weak or too dumb, and I was broken or snapped or beaten—and thereby caused a world or a city or a life to be tortured or extinguished. I felt, in other words, intimate with death's foyer in those snow-bleached hours slogging up that Himalayan facade, dragging behind me a rushed facsimile of a modernist masterwork in a sledge.

As evening fell, and more dangerously as the temperature fell, I neared the designated coordinates of the drop-off. I turned a corner and incredibly I saw—at first I concluded it must be another hallucination—nestled into the rock face a massive structure that looked like exact replicas of the giant Buddhas in Afghanistan's Bamiyan valley. I stood stunned, but no sooner had I begun to wrap my mind around this miracle than I found myself surrounded by twenty heavily armed, masked soldiers who relieved me of the Rauschenberg sculpture.

I must have briefly blacked out, as what I remember next is being dragged toward the Buddhas and then through a maze of hallways of increasingly ornate and voluptuous appointments until I was thrown, not ungently, into a chair (rather ragged and plain relative to the rest of the surroundings), which was turned toward a roaring fire, and I was told, "Mistleto will be with you in a moment."

A moment later she entered. She turned out to be tall and thin, and something about her was familiar. She wore a small mask, but I guessed she was around my age, in her fifties, Asian, perhaps Nepali or Korean. She came in with a tray on which were cups and a thermos of tea. Sitting in a chair next to mine in front of the fire, she said, "Ambassador Yamamoto's children are at this moment being dropped off in front of the U.S. embassy in Bern." Answering my look, she said, "You'll have to take my word for it."

I decided to do so, and therefore, using my tongue, activated the homing signal a Mossad dentist had implanted in a fake rear molar. This gave us forty minutes before the mountain would be obliterated by Tomahawk missiles.

She looked at me in an amused way, making me wonder momentarily if she somehow knew about the signal and the imminent strike. She said:

Several years ago I found myself alone in a far-flung part of the city. I'd left my seven-year-old son with my husband and had come to that area to spend some time in a hotel to quote sort things out.

I hadn't quite had a breakdown, though it felt like one was imminent. My days had been spent sitting listlessly watching my boy play, or, worse, not watching him play and instead staring off into space. Or we'd be at the store or a restaurant or on the street and I'd be seized with a formless anxiety that made me rush home, rudely and desperately, hazardously, and where I'd find little relief but at least an anesthetizing familiarity. At night I suffered badly from insomnia.

I refused doctors or any kind of treatment. That was no doubt a serious mistake—even I understood that—but I couldn't face being that type of failure, no matter if that was the wrong term for it. I'd argued with my husband that the doctors didn't know what they were doing, that the drugs were crude, primitive, worse than the ailment, and that talk therapy was just a long con. While I believed each of these things to be true, privately I knew the real reason I refused that kind of help was because I'd become overly intimate with and somehow comforted by my own rotting, and I had also come to see the illness as inseparable from myself, and, most important if somewhat contradictory, I had felt it to be the necessary preliminary stage before a crucial transformation, perhaps the one I had just made.

The hotel I'd chosen was new but already shabby. It was the first one I'd found when I put in what I was willing to pay. It was close to the airport.

Lying in the hotel bed, I'd fallen asleep quickly, perhaps exhausted by packing and leaving my home. But even while it was happening, the ease with which I was drifting off to sleep amazed me. At that moment I didn't miss my son or my husband, not exactly. On other nights, at that time, we'd be rushing to clean up the dinner table and put everything away for the night while one or then both of us would be helping the boy wash up and get ready for bed.

For a time the sheer labor of living, of getting food to the table and not letting the house descend too much into chaos, had created a momentum within which I didn't have the time or energy to think. But then soon enough I did begin to think. I'd begun a sequence of thoughts—or maybe *sequence* is the wrong word. Maybe it was a stumbling, repeating, knotted tangle of thoughts. But in any case, these *thoughts* had brought me here, outside my home. I fell asleep and my son and my husband were far from my mind, which was taken up with this new, unfamiliar neighborhood I'd now found myself in and the hotel room, ordinary as it was, and the clean stiff cool sheets. I didn't miss my family, or rather the thought of them was a very dull pinching feeling behind my eyes that I successfully ignored until it faded away.

In the morning when I woke up I felt a moment of calm, even of peace. But then, when I thought about the implication—that the peace came in the wake of an abandonment—a surge of guilt came over me and the formless panic that just a moment ago had seemed so far away flooded in and filled the hotel room with a changed air: sharper somehow, with tiny blades that tore at you as you breathed and as you moved through space. I focused on the view.

The view was expansive and, at first, in the night, I'd thought somehow I was looking over the water. But I quickly realized—and this was confirmed in the morning—that my view was of one of those huge cemeteries that lie hidden within the city.

The cemetery was across a highway from the hotel. My room was a dozen flights up, and I could peer over acres of graves, in fact I could see all the way to where the city began again, beyond a thickish row of trees, and the cluster of downtown skyscrapers in the distance could become, with very little imagination, simply grander sepulchers.

I saw trees among the rows of graves and picked out one dark green leafy maple and stared at it for a long time: this moment it was still, this moment it fluttered violently, this moment its branches swayed in a slow tidal rhythm.

I got up to make some coffee.

The cheap machine gurgled and produced a measly amount of watery stuff. The room was overly cold, and the pleasurable feeling of the hot cup made me realize this and woke me more than the beverage's obscure amount of caffeine.

I spent days, perhaps weeks this way. And then some noise made me eventually leave the hotel. An intense noise, that of a huge crowd.

At first I thought, in my distraction, I'd missed some national event—maybe a sports victory for which the city was celebrating in a massive ticker tape parade. In a sense I was right; however, it wasn't a parade, not exactly.

It was a protest, a huge and general one, against the excesses of corporations.

Their many sins were bullet-pointed on homemade placards: climate disasters, of which the varieties were sub-listed (drought, floods, fire, storms, famine, lost species and cities); the purchasing of politicians; war profiteering; carcinogens in our food; the overmilitarized police force;

covert and overt racism; mass incarceration and disenfran-
chisement; the calculated intentional impoverishment of a
working class; the nonstop production of sweet moral an-
esthesia for the consumer class; alienation; triumphalism;
ugliness; etc. The usual list. But this time, for whatever
reason—maybe it was the weather or the upcoming war or
the lingering ongoing one—more and more people were
taking to the streets to protest.

It had grown out of a smaller action the previous day. An
environmental activist had been killed by a private army.
She and others had been barricading the road to a shale
development site. In the middle of the night the mercenaries
had come and attacked, scattering the group. In the battle
this young woman had been clubbed and died of a head injury. It had helped, it was said, that the woman was white
and a "telegenic corpse." For whatever reason her death was
a trigger.

I joined the crowd.

I hated and mistrusted mobs and crowds, but for the
moment, in this anonymous flow, I felt invisible, more a
ghost. But as time passed, I sensed pockets of fear and anger ready to detonate.

The growing horde marched down a wide avenue and
took over a public square. For a while people just stood,
milling about the square, waiting. There was the sense that
the thing this mass was going to destroy—whether store-
fronts, cars, offices, monuments, city hall—was collectively

being decided upon, telepathically, even as people just stood or talked or spread leaflets or gave speeches or chanted.

I felt this process happening, but I wasn't interested in it. Not yet. For a long time I didn't care about the goal of the crowd, just that it was. For the moment I simply walked through it, a ghost, looking at faces.

Just then I was no longer looking for certain basic characteristics. I was no longer engaged in a deeply habitual and immediately reductive profiling, looking to see if a person had signs of wealth or if they were beautiful, sorting by fashion and race and age, instantly categorizing people into fuckable or non, wealthy or non, working class or non, enviable or non, pitiful or non.

But here, in the protesting crowd, as a ghost, I began seeing faces in a completely different way. I saw them as simply faces—divorced from context. Or, that the context had become so general. I saw the crowd as if it were a howling animal asking out loud if it was going to die or suffer forever or if, after a final anguished spasm, it was going to find relief by becoming something else entirely. And for some reason this allowed me to see each face clearly. And all the faces were beautiful and sad. Waiting, ignorant, expectant—but crushable. Innocent of but therefore most vulnerable to destruction.

I passed hours and then days this way, the crowd not dispersing but growing larger, more permanent, with systems of rest and shelter and food emerging. And I simply walked and walked through the crowd, hundreds and thousands of faces, all beautiful and all sad. Face after face after face after face. The evident sadness and beauty made me try to hunt out the happy and the ugly, to seek out the joyful or deformed or mismatched—but each time I thought I saw someone like this, the proof of their happiness evaporated. And their ugliness, too.

After ten days, in the small hours of the morning, troops invaded the square. Flash bombs, rubber bullets and tear gas and then real bullets. The crowd responded momentarily with rocks and bottles. There was a stampede and blood. I saw an old woman get trampled.

Now I was no longer a ghost but one of them, running and scared.

Strangely, it was at that moment, in the initial fleeing, that I saw my husband and son. They were walking quickly fifty feet away in another direction from mine. I recognized their clothing. It was just a moment, but that, as much as the mayhem, resubstantiated me, unghosted me.

I found myself running with about six others. We'd fled the square at the same time, immediately, and then broke off from the larger throng through a side street. As we slowed to a walk we looked at one another and began laughing, though we were feeling ashamed. We'd escaped easily; we'd dispersed at the very first sign.

But then the signals began coming, first through our devices and then by shout. The protest was reconvening, evolving. We, the protesters, were now, so said these messages, going to sabotage and occupy. These directives to sabotage or occupy were premeditated but competing messages. The police action had evidently been seen as inevitable, and many diverse cells had been planning their countermoves for some time.

The rioters, the destroyers, the saboteurs—a general class made up of several groups at various levels of organization and militancy—were rising as flash mobs to attack the stock exchange, prisons, and banks. They were burning cars and homes but only in select, symbolically affluent, neighborhoods. They used blunt instruments, simple but potent explosives, and fire. Some, the most effective, were surgical and quick: doing maximum property damage to emblematic institutions, making sure to maintain their anonymity, and fading quickly into the night. They inspired terror in the dominant class (even if the property damage was erased overnight by a tactically hyper-responsive team of contractors). In the end it was the diversity of targets, so many and so spread out across the city (and in fact the number was further proof of the hegemony's power and success), that prevented even the massive resources of the police state from effectively responding to this epidemic of riot.

Instead of continuing my retreat back to the hotel, this new call spurred me to action. I decided to join those using the second tactic, the occupiers. I admit that I was probably motivated by shame at my cowardice, which had been so apparent in my initial reaction to the state's show of power.

I scanned the constantly updating message boards and realized one of the larger occupying groups was targeting a nearby skyscraper, the headquarters of a global energy company. I headed over.

As I approached initially I was taken aback by the lack of police presence.

Usually and of course even more robustly than the courthouse, parliamentary buildings, and schools—that is, those buildings necessary for a working democracy—structures such as this corporate flagship, banks, brokerage offices, and the stock exchange would have been protected by flanks of security personnel. (It is painfully obvious that during these times of mayhem the cultural buildings, the museums and libraries, have no security whatsoever.) The number of protesters must be truly enormous, I thought, if security personnel have been diverted from such central targets. However, as I approached, I realized my mistake. There *were* legions of riot cops and rows of armored vehicles, noise cannons, and prison vans, but they were set up at a distance, to the side. I was terrified at the sight of them, but something in me, along with a steady and swelling crowd, pushed me forward toward the building.

The police didn't stop our flow, and, seeing an opportunity, we surged ahead.

We quickly took over the boulevard and with a general cheer crashed into the skyscraper's lobby. Our collective steps satisfyingly crunched over shattered glass.

We felt victorious—but should have known better.

At first I thought the cops were just overwhelmed and unwilling to confront such a huge segment of the public, but it became all too clear that the state had planned at least as elaborately as the protesters. (Later it was even suggested that the entire ambition to take that particular building had been planted by agents provocateurs.) As dawn broke the next day, it slowly became clear to us that we'd been tricked into imprisoning ourselves.

The police surrounded the building. Emergency powers given to the courts had, overnight, accused and convicted and sentenced all of us. We'd been found guilty of a long and somewhat arbitrary list of crimes: property damage, resisting arrest, theft, jaywalking, littering, reckless endangerment, treason. The details mattered little, as the consequences were the same no matter the exact definition of the offense. The police announced that if citizens voluntarily surrendered they would be transferred to a standard corporate labor camp (where, we knew, prisoners would spend the rest of their lives doing monotonous low-level data analysis in exchange for their consumer spending units and daily gruel). If we didn't surrender, the police continued, we would be sentenced to capital punishment; that is, they claimed, they would blow up the building.

About half the occupants chose to go to the corporate labor camps, saying they preferred the dead soul grind of the computer monitor and the Siberian cubicle seas to death penalty by high-rise demolition. Sick at heart, we watched them stream steadily out all morning.

The remainder had decided to call the state's bluff. We were still a large number, and if they did indeed blow up the building and commit mass murder, there was little doubt a large enough number of martyrs would be created and so a real risk would be run of initiating a powerful recruiting vehicle for the resistance. However, that left us under siege. A nervous few days passed. Power had been cut off from the building and slowly our devices became useless. We were without news or communication from or to the outside world.

Eventually a general meeting was convened on one of the upper floors, which had previously housed the energy company's employee café. (Later, we'd learn that in return for their headquarters being converted into an extemporaneous prison for the occupying protesters, the energy company received massive tax subsidies, which enabled them to build a tower of rivaling height only a few blocks away.) At that meeting it was decided that rather than wait for our own execution, and better than sitting and starving, we would organize ourselves.

Our objective would not only be, we said, survival, but a bolder and more defiant goal. We would once again refashion the occupation, which the state had transformed into an incarceration, and make it into a utopian colony founded on principles of equality, collective decision making, cooperative labor, and shared property.

The first months were the most difficult, but we survived on rodent meat as well as the seemingly inexhaustible supply of vending machine nuts and candy bars cached throughout the acres of open-plan office space. Things improved considerably when the communication subcommittee established, through Morse coded mirror transmissions, carrier pigeon, and semaphore signals, a regular helicopter drop of essential supplies. These were provided either by a sympathetic resistance group on the outside or, as the suspicious among us deemed more likely, directly by the state, which hoped to keep us from acts of desperation as well as to wait out the media interest in our story.

We lasted this way for several years.

What ended our experiment in alternative living was, sadly, not a final showdown or a dramatic escape but simply the short attention span of the state. Or, to be more accurate, in the end our ability to leave the skyscraper came about through a cost-benefit analysis, run by ruthless corporate-government actuaries, which showed any potential asset loss incurred by granting us geographic mobility was heavily and decisively outweighed by the debt incurred in the continuing wages paid and resources spent to hold us captive.

In other words, we weren't worth it.

One day we woke to realize the police were no longer guarding us. And while I'd like to report otherwise, at that time no one, including myself, brought up the argument of staying. The moral logic for communal living was abstractly very persuasive, but we'd soon discovered the pressure to conform to the needs of the group had become, even for the most aggressively righteous among us, insidiously stifling and unbearable.

It took a relatively short time to reenter the larger society. I returned to my hotel by the airport that overlooked the gigantic graveyard. The dark green leaves of my chosen maple tree still swayed in slow tidal rhythm. And across the street the dead had not moved.

And then Ms. Mistleto stopped talking. I felt the heat from the fireplace and my fingers and toes were tingling as they thawed. In the distance I thought I heard an alarm. Ms. Mistleto smiled and said that she looked forward to working with me, and then she stood and in a swift motion sprayed tear gas directly into my eyes.

Her movement was so sudden I didn't have time to turn and was blinded. When I partly recovered, just a half minute later, I saw a wall had swung open to reveal secret stairs. I sprinted after her but was too late as I saw Mistleto speeding away on a motorcycle through tunnelworks that no doubt took her through an elaborately capable and planned getaway. I barely had time to curse and take cover before the Tomahawk missiles I'd ordered came raining down in a catastrophic and thunderous torrent.

Curses

One night during my first year in New York, I went on a whim to an art opening. I was as alone then as I am now, but the difference was I didn't know I'd always be. Those years were exciting because I was sure some friendship, some *relief,* was just around the corner. Hidden in the next book, whispered in tomorrow's film or song. At the next party.

I was standing in front of a painting when I felt someone come and stand next to me.

It was Frank's sister. I vaguely knew who she was because of her brother. And later, I'd learn that Frank's money was behind the gallery, which was why they were both there.

I stepped back so she was just a little between myself and the painting. A third person joined us, and Frank's sister said the following to him.

What was strange was that something in her voice—maybe its bitterness, its hissing, a kind of hot contempt one understood was lifelong—reminded me uncannily of Vu. So that, even though I suspected we had more or less forgotten about each other, and even though up to that moment Vu had felt far far away—suddenly he was here.

The voice said:

Everywhere there is no there there. Except for those and that that's fucked. There there's hell. Detroit, Dharavi, Guryong Village, Cova da Moura, Oakland.

You don't have to believe me when I say I'm done. I've more than enough in it for both our fuck-yous even as they collide.

No, I will not calm down and—

No I am not drunk!

I thought my brother was good, noble. But as we've grown older, it's not that the hypocrisies have become more evident. I mean, all our hypocrisies have become more evident, so it isn't that. It's that first of all, how easily he shrugs off the hypocrisy, as if it's nothing, nothing really, as if to say, What could one really do about it? Circumstances have forced me to become a parasite. There's really no choice. *So that's the first thing. How easily he shrugs it off, which is repulsive to me, disgusting to me. But the final thing, the main thing, the true reason I can't stand him, is because he reminds me of me.*

He thinks this is all okay because the money cleans it. No, he wouldn't say so directly. But it's what he believes. The money makes it clean and young and beautiful. And it does! It does make it all clean and beautiful and young!

I used to worship him, but now I can't stand him.

I should say, I can't stand him, because I used to worship him.

I'll be short.

I'll be short but not because my fury is exhausted, but because it is modular, a flat piece. A segment you can re-peat endlessly. Until you understand it is the floor upon which all existence sits, and which is infernal.

Now we're all Icarus. Cyborgs with our wings. An aug-mented reality. The Cassandra warnings forgotten. And it's always on, always simultaneous: the soaring and the panic, spasm and grace, flight and fall.

Burn it to the ground.

Burn it to the motherfucking ground.

And then Frank's sister stopped and immediately walked out of the gallery. Her interlocutor simply moved away and started looking at another painting as if nothing had happened.

I stood in an envelope of unexpected silence, bewil-dered and bereft by my friend's sudden, so to speak, ap-pearance and then disappearance, in the form of Frank's sister's curses. *Where is Vu?* I wondered.

And then impulsively I ran out and went after Frank's sister, determined suddenly that she was going to become if not a friend then some kind of accomplice.

Dear Cyborgs,

Today's puzzler. For once the way is clear. No scare quotes. No doubt. Oh, but the flesh is weak! And the door is closing closing . . .

Ever,

It's easier to imagine the end of the world than

A few hours later I went at the regular time to the karaoke bar to meet Muriel and Dave. The bar, which had several names but usually went by Alibi, took up the entire ninth floor of a hastily built structure amid the dirty neon of one of Diaspora City's seedier districts. A heavy-pile, regal red carpet covered the floor of the stage, which was illuminated with several bare low-watt bulbs. As usual that night it was crowded and filled with clinks and respectful low murmurs. I found Dave at a table nursing a tequila.

As I sat down he pointed across the room. Muriel was waiting next to the stage and was about to go on and sing. A stylish Sri Lankan we knew named Bill was just finishing up a plaintive version of "Rubber Ring" by the Smiths. When Bill finished, Muriel stepped onto the stage and took the microphone. Her accompaniment began and from the opening strum of guitar I immediately knew she'd chosen one of her old standbys, namely "물 좀 주소" (Gimme Some Water) by Han Dae-soo. While she was singing, Dave leaned over and told me he'd gone home, had dinner, and then took a short nap. During which, he said, he'd had the most disquieting dream.

"In my dream," Dave whispered, "I was a junior member of a theater company. We were putting on a play in which the main character was the devil. The devil in the play was supposed to be very seductive and charismatic, and one conceit of the drama was that he simultaneously won over not only the other characters but the members of the audience as well.

"I was the understudy to the actor who played the devil.

"The actor who played the devil happened to be fantastic. He had that internal light sometimes spoken of in actors, which he could brighten or dim at will, and which made him incredibly charming and mesmerizing to watch. I didn't mind so much being this actor's understudy, and, what's more, I thought there was a great deal I could learn from him.

"Each night during our run of this play, the other understudies and bits of the crew and cast would gather in a small room at the back of the theater. There we'd watch the performance on a closed-circuit TV monitor.

"In my dream the actual devil was also part of our company, and he would join us in this room to watch the performance.

"He had wanted to play himself, but everyone had agreed that the other actor would do a better job.

"The devil was incensed by this. And he would come to the performances and join us in the small room and talk to the television set—or us or himself, no one was sure who he was talking to—and complain loudly and bitterly that the actor onstage was a hack and a phony, that he didn't know why we'd chosen this actor over himself, that the performance was terrible, that if you wanted someone to play the devil, why, he was the perfect and natural choice! And on and on, each night, the devil would complain like this.

"Soon we were all sick and tired of the devil's moaning and bellyaching.

"And one night the director actually joined us to watch backstage. And as the devil went into his usual tirade, the director, who was hearing it for the first time, grew increasingly angry and red-faced until finally she exploded and shouted at him, *Fine! You're such a pain in the ass. Tomorrow's matinee*—you *play the role.*

"And the devil smiled broadly, and you could see how wonderfully pleased he was with himself.

"But then the next day he went on in front of a quarter-full house—and the devil was just awful at playing himself. He was crabby and ungraceful and whiny, just as he'd been all along, the entire time we'd known him (which seemed like forever), and so he was totally unconvincing as the seductive embodiment of sly evil he was supposed to be portraying.

"Watching the tiny monitor, everyone in the room at the back of the theater laughed and jeered and then grew smugly quiet as the devil made a fool of himself onstage. I, however, never made a peep and I didn't laugh or shout at the devil on the monitor like the others. I just sat there and thought, *When will I be given a chance?* And also I thought, *I guess it's true what they say: the squeaky wheel is always the one that gets the grease.*"

Dave stopped talking as there was an explosion of whistles and hoots as Muriel drove the folk song through its final verse. As usual she was giving it her all, which the audience evidently appreciated, begging for more when she finished. Muriel was happy to comply, and after quickly programming the karaoke machine for her next number, we heard a sweet, sad piano phrase, and I could tell she was going to sing another of her favorites: "Auch kleine Dinge können uns entzücken" (Even Little Things Can Delight Us) by Hugo Wolf.

These performances came to her naturally and were minutes we downplayed as simpler, even gauche entertainment—but they also held, in their nugget of fantasy, a surprising sustenance. The effects on her of these seemingly minor acts of self-actualization were, I'd noticed, remarkably durable. Maybe Dave, in his own way, had noticed the same, but the observation in him had triggered something different, a desire to also be recognized, thus his dream. Or so I interpreted it. I decided to encourage him. "You should go up," I said, "and sing."

"Me? No, I couldn't."

"Sure you could. Why not?"

"Hmm," he said, noncommittally, but I could tell the seed of the idea had been planted. That was enough for now, I decided, and we turned our attention once again to Muriel, who was capable of handling Wolf's lieder—no one could argue otherwise—with an outstanding delicacy. Nonetheless, as I'd heard her sing night after night for so many years, my attention wandered a bit, and I scanned the various rapt faces in the crowd. The Alibi always held an eclectic bunch, reflective of the nature of Diaspora City, and seeing it this night stirred up a thought that had been agitating in the background for my attention, a fundamental aporia that seemed to distort all my days here.

I leaned toward Dave and, hoping not to appear rude by talking during our friend's performance (but she wasn't paying any attention to us; when she was singing Muriel was truly transported to a different dimension), said, "The thing about this corridor of our city—from Woodside and Jackson Heights through Elmhurst through Corona through Flushing and on to Bayside and beyond—an incredible swath, at times like the Kowloon Walled City in its density and inventive bricolage, and by far superseding it in terms of the sheer diversity of its immigrant populations, is that this often-praised mixing shoulder-to-shoulder of people from every dominion on the planet breeds a respectful and intimate but insuperable separation, which is made all the more vexing due to proximity.

"In the morning one can see the parents of—among many others—Sikh children and Uruguayan children, Romanian children and Cameroonian children, Bhutanese children and Basque children, all dropping off their kids at the elementary school. One perhaps cannot imagine such a sight without experiencing it firsthand. The place is awash in color of both traditional costumes and very au courant if off-the-rack business casual; the Gujarati-inflected English mixes with scrubbed Midwestern and lilting Cantonese as I hear striver family heads discussing playdates and swapping recipes. Nowhere else on earth does this prismatic confluence occur.

"And yet for its singularity, everyone is rather ho-hum about the spectacle. The smoothing of all that difference into capitalist civility is remarkably unremarked upon. Oh, the omnipotent digestive juices of the market's gut—it eats it all! And maybe the nonremarking is but one other aspect of the digestive process. (How quietly it eats!) So it's true that one, in a moment of weakness, could think it a commercial for American utopia and racial harmony: the interlocking of all these communities, the painless and insidious assimilation, the simultaneous proud and painful resistance to that assimilation, the flow of first to second to third and fourth generations, the seemingly unifying and seemingly ubiquitous materialist ambitions. And yet like the city itself the complex is unknowable, one's neighbors are so close yet so far away, we each find ourselves alone and apart, and the functioning diversity miracle itself is only another demonstration of how far short even the most miraculous must fall from our dreams of them."

I paused as Muriel finished her second song and the room again convulsed in raucous applause. She waited with great showmanship before beginning her concluding number: "Immigrant Song" by Led Zeppelin. Upon hearing the first notes the crowd went wild.

I had to shout in order to be heard but leaned closer to

Dave and yelled, "And yet at other times—when I trundle down its streets and avenues, weary from my day's labors or the prospect of my nightly ones, when I am going to the greengrocer for bell peppers and onion to make another basic bachelor's supper, when I stop to hear the busker's tambourine for just a minute before shyly dropping in a few coins, when I order some sweet meat over rice from the food trucks, when I'm in line to buy Band-Aids and deodorant at the pharmacy—at these times I look around and see all my harried neighbors doing the same, the gimpy and spry, ill- and sweet-tempered, nebbish and vampy, and yes, it's then I do believe in some unity of purpose, despite the chaotic provenances of Diaspora City, and I see the essential program provided to all is not to acquire or win but rather is just to exist—and to avoid pain—and we are not at all making the world and are therefore not at all responsible, but in the moment have only been given it, the prospect and circumstance of the hour, and we are forced to navigate this place, each of us, as best we can.

"Then I think: Fellows! Sisters! Cousins!

"But," I concluded, "the feelings then, while not marked so much by loneliness, are drenched with a resembling error, namely self-pity."

"I think I know *exactly* what you mean," yelled Dave in response. The music had finished and the admiring crowd was giving Muriel a standing ovation, above which it was a struggle to be heard. We were both standing and clapping like the others albeit a tad more mechanically.

Dave said, "Yes, I think I understand you perfectly. I had recently a very similar thought. I'd met this guy at a bar who happened to be a night guard at the Frick museum, and he said he could, since he knew I was a painter ('Only a Sunday painter,' I'd said; 'Whatever,' this guy'd said), if I was interested, let me in to the museum after hours.

"So he set it up," Dave continued, "somehow with his bosses. He was a gregarious guy who was difficult to say no to. And so one night after closing I met him at the museum around ten o'clock and he gave me the run of the place.

"Henry Clay Frick, the man who had collected all these works by Dürer and by Delacroix, these paintings by Watteau and Kirchner, at the time he had collected them was dubbed the most hated man in America. For he was a vicious capitalist, and it would be as if Dick Cheney and Jeffrey Skilling and the Koch brothers were one man and had begun collecting all the Donald Judds and Robert Smithsons and all the Joan Mitchells and Julie Mehretus and all the Joanne Greenbaums and Paul Chans as a historical machine, a timeless massager of their reputations, so that instead of a villainous and rapacious, murderous bigotry and egotism, we instead only remembered dimly this rough history, seen through a glass darkly, and it is as if we were blinkered and blinded by these beautiful and profound works of art placed before our eyes to shield these evil men of power from true and righteous judgment and to shield us, too, from the wearisome task of carrying out that judgment. See—I'm winded just saying so.

"And so I was ecstatic to be allowed into the museum, this mansion, at night when I could roam its halls and peer at these paintings as if I owned them myself, or, even more, as if I were in some cosmic dance with them, some intimate relationship with these nineteenth-century masterpieces, these works by Fragonard and Whistler, these works by Vermeer and Constable, by Goya and Titian, by El Greco and Ingres. And it was, initially, a sublime, sweet, and slow walk through its intimate galleries and down its halls—the museum at night.

"But after a few hours of this, after living out the fantasy of being alone with these paintings, I realized there was something immensely lonely about the experience, or that it was something so ecstatic it had to be savored jointly, with some other soul or souls, or else the solitude would ruin the taste, would transform the sweet into bitter, the wine into vinegar. So I left the museum, came out into the cool night, and walked for hours and hours digesting what I had seen, my mind overrun and seized with both beauty and sadness.

"At dawn I came up with a plan. This was, I recognized, a high point in my life. I couldn't just leave it (which I realize now was perhaps unwise), and I thought: I have to do it *again*. But this time I have to *bring somebody else*.

"And so I invited this woman I knew.

"She happened to be an art critic. Actually she was an arts *blogger*. Well, in actual fact, she was a data analyst at a corporation and worked eighty hours a week building profiles of you and me and everyone else we know so that targeted messages would have us buy, at just the right moment, just the right brand of diaper or automobile or colonoscopy. For her tireless efforts she was paid huge sums with which she bought the combinations of Xanax and marijuana and cocaine and vodka that helped to ease her often ruffled psyche. But in a previous incarnation she had held down waitressing and dog-walking jobs so that she could get through an MFA in studio art, in 'multimedia,' which she claimed was a vocation—and this turned out to be true—for which she had no calling.

"However, these days, on the side—because she was immensely talented and energetic, which was why I was drawn to her—she contributed (under pseudonym) to one of the city's more widely read art blogs. She made it a point to spend all of her scarce free time going to galleries. In fact, this was where I'd met her, standing in front of a painting we both happened to admire. We casually exchanged comments ('mesmerizing,' 'so beautiful,' 'makes it look easy') and that was that—but then her face popped up several weeks later on OKCupid.

"So a month after my first visit to the Frick my friend quite generously arranged for it to happen again. Except this time I was bringing along a date.

"At first it was just as before but better, because it was still a fantastic privilege to wander that space and live for a few hours with those paintings in a bubble of private intimacy, but it was even *better* because one could share that wonder with another person, and so that wonder—

the ecstasy, the joy—became reflected and built up by some harmonic into a golden, gonging mutual pleasure.

"But she kept talking.

"She talked the entire time. And it wasn't that what she was saying was so wrong or so pedantic or so pandering or so not up-to-the-moment. These things were true. But they were true about what I was saying also. And I, too, was talking the whole time. We were commenting on our experience, and the exegesis, which was necessary to make the sublime more human, more touchable, turned out to be the thing that tarnished it irreparably, secularized it if not made it profane, and so turned the transcendent ritual into a bauble of anecdote.

"Fucked alone. And if not alone, likewise fucked," concluded Dave.

By this time Muriel had made her way off the stage and slid through the shadows to join us at our table. She'd caught the tail end of Dave's anecdote.

For a while no one said anything, and we all turned toward the stage to listen to a Tuvan family throat-singing in subtle harmony.

After a moment, however, Muriel leaned toward me to say out of the side of her mouth, "Before I forget, here's your book," and she took my lost novel out of her bag and slid it toward me. "You left it at the Thai restaurant where we'd had lunch."

"Oh, great! I was looking for that. I thought I'd left it at home." I took the Inspector Tate mystery novel from her and put it on the chair beside me.

Then Muriel turned to Dave and said, "By the way, I know precisely what you mean. *Precisely!* Progress: so-called! The more things change, the goddamn more the même chose no doubt. Am I right or am I right. What you say reminds me of a very similar thing that happened to me where I work. In the hospital complex there's a cafeteria space that keeps changing. It's in an out-of-the-way section of the hospital, which is why I liked it. It's two blocks away from my ward, so I figured I probably wouldn't see anyone I knew. I like to preserve my privacy. And also, since it seems an out-of-the-way area, not just for me but for almost everybody, it was often empty.

"There *is* an ophthalmology wing close by. You can tell because the only people you'd see in the cafeteria were men and women with a white, gauzy patch over one eye, always huddled over a bag of chips or a basket of wilting French fries. But other than these depressed cyclops I more or less had the cafeteria to myself.

"Which was the problem, because as the huge cafeteria space was always empty, it didn't quite make sense to keep the place going. On the other hand, it was in an awkward location, which I imagine made repurposing it difficult. It was that fact plus managerial inertia that allowed the cyclops and me to continue to have our chips and tuna melts and greasy chicken noodle soup and watery coffee in peace for so long. But it couldn't last forever. Nothing does, goes the rule.

"The cafeteria area has gone through three major upheavals since I've worked at the hospital. This was how

I'd found it initially, and it was the best for me, but it was no doubt doomed because this version reeked, literally, of inefficient subsidies and a cheap, bulk mind: mushy lasagna and vats of tomato-bean soup and grainy cheese macaroni. Plastic trays and a deep fryer and Jell-O desserts. You get the idea. The workers looked bored out of their minds; however, there were more than a dozen of them. The dreary seating area was purely functional, but in the afternoon this could be offset by a flood of soft warm sunlight. I would happily go there on my breaks to drink their bad coffee and read my book and even sometimes stopped for an hour just to unwind after my shift.

"But inevitably the cafeteria became too great a financial burden. Not enough cyclopes paid to eat its grilled cheese sandwiches and soggy vegetables. So I was saddened but also not surprised when I went one day and found the place had been shuttered. The dozen workers had moved on, presumably, and I barely registered the notion that I'd most likely never see them again. I was frankly more pained to see the darkened lights over the grill, the tarped cashier's register, and the dusty gloom in front of which a sign had been placed: THIS AREA CLOSED.

"For several months I didn't go back. Instead I tried to find different places for my breaks: a Chinese restaurant, the steps outside the library, the park. Each of these, I found, was an imperfect place to rest. The park wouldn't work on cold or windy days. I had to be in the mood for Chinese food to justify the visit to Wok and Roll. And the library steps were okay, but crowded with teenagers. So after weeks and months of some restless roaming, one day I wandered back over.

"I was surprised to see an entirely different cafeteria had sprung up, a more upscale one. The new place featured fashionable baked goods and soups and juices. The coffee, too, had improved, though everything had also doubled in price. There were fewer workers, but they seemed at first happier, or perhaps they were better paid.

"Initially I was annoyed. The once dreary seating area had become a designed space with color-coordinated furniture and decorations of tasteful kitsch. However, I found myself growling less when I realized it still adequately functioned as a place of rest. It's true my small meals had doubled in price, and I was slightly ill at ease sitting underneath reindeer antlers painted sky blue or beside the polished fender of what a prominent sign informed came from a 1956 Cadillac Eldorado Biarritz, but I could eventually tune out this visual noise when I realized that, in general, it was still just me and the glaucoma-diseased and the cataract-addled—that is, once again it was only me and the cyclopes. It's true a few more young, mostly foreign, doctors could be found there, usually in pairs or in threes, but these were actually rare sightings, despite these people no doubt being the establishment's intended clientele.

"So I settled back into my routine, coming to the new cafeteria on my lunch breaks and after work. It was here I thought about my paintings and it was here that I would sometimes do some drawings. I found refuge once again in the now-gentrified space, slurping my upmarket beverage and tucking into my line-caught albacore tuna chunk sandwich made with artisanal levain—financially poorer but spiritually enriched, I concluded, through sanctuary. My depressed cyclopes looked the same, perhaps a smidgen droopier, but that was probably accounted for by the contrast between them and their shiny, optimistic surroundings.

"Gradually, however, the perky owners and employees (it was difficult, at a glance, to tell them apart) of the new café began looking a little tired, more harried and shopworn. It took me a few weeks to figure out why this was so, but eventually it hit me: the business was failing. The expected legion of young, hip doctors and their capitulating cohorts had failed to appear. My interludes there were still peaceful, but marred slightly as *Not too long from now,* I predicted with some certainty, *the cyclopes and I will once again be homeless.*

"But for months and months it kept not happening. It was as if the owners of the gentrified cafeteria could not themselves believe in their own defeat. But the telltale signs kept appearing. There were desperate menu changes: bacon hot dogs and fondue flights. Near the touchscreen cash register, the owner had displayed a sequelless children's book she'd authored titled *We Opened a Restaurant!*

"Yet in time and inevitably, their defeat conquered their disbelief of it, and this second version of the cafeteria also closed. It seemed to happen even more unceremoniously, as if in shame, and over a weekend the place was stripped nearly to its studs.

"Where the cyclopes went I did not know, but I began another bout of wandering. From the shrimp-garlic lunch special at Double Happiness to the wet park benches over to the teenage riots of the public library—I made my unhappy rounds. But eventually, out of nostalgia or weariness I couldn't tell you, I returned.

"I suspect mostly it was to grieve the passing of the two cafeterias and not to see if yet another version had since come into being. If you had asked me at the time I would have said it was much too soon, but—there it was: a *third* version of the cafeteria. However, this time it was something I was wholly unprepared for or (perhaps should have been but) in no way expected.

"In a corner along the wall two open refrigerated display cases contained an assortment of prepackaged sandwiches and wraps and salads. They looked as flavorful as cold iceberg lettuce, which is what most of the sandwiches seemed to be made out of. A separate shelf had urns of passable (corporate, familiar) coffee. Another case displayed bags of chips and plastic-looking fruit. All of this was compressed into one small section of the cafeteria.

"I'd filled a paper cup of coffee and was momentarily confused as to how to pay for it when I realized that a quartet of monoliths, which I'd subconsciously ignored when I'd passed them, because they were too unfathomable, were actually checkout robots. A sign explained that by removing the cup from the area, the price of a small coffee would automatically be deducted from my bank account, which somehow the monoliths had already spoken to and from which they had received approval for payment. If I had any questions about the transaction I could ask the digitized cafeteria's sole human employee, whose only other task that I could surmise seemed to be refilling the coffee urns.

"I took my cup over to the seating area, which was now larger and filled with indestructible-looking modular seating. Not entirely uncomfortable, nonetheless there was something authoritarian in the seating that suggested tarrying over your turkey wrap any longer than half an hour would be unseemly.

"But the most surprising thing of all was that the place was packed. Conversation rattled the air as nurses and doctors nodded over coffee or hunched over laptops. And all about these, my dear cyclopes dotted the scene, uncharacteristically grinning, like drugged morons, over their shiny, burst bags of potato chips.

"It was so crowded that I couldn't find a peaceful seat. I just threw out my full cup of coffee and left and have never been back," concluded Muriel.

After Muriel had stopped talking, the three of us just sat quietly for some time. Maybe her tale had depressed us a little.

In fact, the three of us didn't talk much more that evening, but after several hours had passed, just at the very end of our night out, and after many tequilas, we prevailed on Dave to take a try at singing. He nervously went up to the stage to a smattering but supportive applause. He'd chosen "Yesterday" by the Beatles and the Eagles' "Hotel California"—and he performed very passable versions of both of these.

End-User License Agreement

After the karaoke bar I stumbled home, rather drunk, and fell into a dead sleep. An hour or two later, however, I woke up thirsty and with a terrible headache. I got up to drink a glass of water and then lay back in bed, but found I was unable to sleep. Instead I again thought of Ms. Mistleto.

After losing her in the catacombs beneath the Himalayas, the next time I met her was when it was discovered she was behind a major cyberattack against our government.

The president, several members of Congress, and two Supreme Court justices had had their emails and drives compromised. In addition to the usual infidelities and sex trafficking, the drug habits and corporate kickbacks, it was deemed most embarrassingly revealed that these politicians were atrocious hobbyists. Several of them wrote confessional poetry, two were authors of soft-porn fan fiction, and the president himself painted psychoanalytically revealing self-portraits in which he unintentionally confessed he was a child-man, a buffoon manipulated by devious puppet masters.

The CIA decided this information could never become public, and so a massive effort was made to find the hacker and hide the evidence. Elaborate counterstories were concocted, witnesses disappeared, and journalists were paid off. Years later bits came out, and the president's paintings even were revealed—but by that time the danger had passed and in any event his incompetence was less a state secret than an oddly effective ingredient of his charisma. Nonetheless, at the time a fortune in resources was spent on a tremendous hunt to find the guilty party.

Slowly we realized (or she let us realize) that the person behind these crafty invasions of privacy was Ms. Mistleto.

One night a few weeks after I'd been briefed on the situation I found myself in the town of Mostar in Bosnia-Herzegovina. Our intel said Ms. Mistleto was holed up in a tower connected to an ancient bridge there. I approached the thickly walled tower via a scramble up a steep bank. A cold breeze shot across the river, and the air smelled of a mix of moss and limestone.

I scaled the structure and entered the tower through a window where I saw Ms. Mistleto standing in a shaft of moonlight with her back turned to me. I was about to reach for my raygun, but then felt a prick on the side of my neck. "I've developed," Mistleto suddenly said, "an interesting derivative of the Amazonian drug curare, which as you know paralyzes the muscles." I slumped to the floor, unable to move.

Ms. Mistleto said:

After I got out of jail I wanted to find my family, but they'd moved and no one knew where they were. I'd been away, and people were not particularly forthcoming to an ex-con and a woman who'd abandoned her family.

Losing everything does gift you with freedom if nothing else. That's a rewrite of a pithier song refrain.

Eventually—and this wasn't easy and depended not a little upon the kindness of strangers and the welfare state— I found an apartment. And under a false name I got a job at the same energy company I'd protested against years ago. In their terrifyingly similar, newer building I worked cleaning bathrooms and offices on the night crew. No one wanted to unionize; they paid a decent wage.

I'd come home and collapse each night at four in the morning. But I'd be up at ten. And then I would spend the daytime hours in the apartment, motionless in the summer heat, listening to muted sounds from my neighbors. And I'd try to raise the energy to begin looking for my husband and son. Or I'd think about trying to raise the energy to do so, what that might entail. They were out there and I could find them. The question was did I have the strength and did they want to be found. My son would be a teenager by now. And so I would spot other kids, thirteen or fifteen, in groups or alone, defiant or sweet, handsome or lopsided, usually looking at their phones—and I'd wonder where he was, my son.

It was a criminal thing I'd done, cruel and selfish—and I suffered from shame. But part of me also felt it had been someone else, that I had been someone else. And that whoever that insane person was, she'd been transformed by time and prison. I was now someone less selfish and troubled, someone who wanted only a small, regular life.

But part of *raising the energy* to look for my son was recognizing this was bullshit. I had been that insane person. And I was just as selfish and troubled. Though all I wanted now—that part was true—was a small and regular life.

My husband was different. I felt less guilt about that. Not no guilt but less. Our marriage had been dying. When I left it was less a therapeutic time-out than a divorce in all but name.

And he was a good man, stable, less moody and more practical than I. He, I also knew—despite my wanting very much to think otherwise—would provide a better home for our son than I could. That was the justification for my selfishness. It was meager but I lived off it. At times, if I had anything, this was all I had.

So why should I bother them after all this time?

It kept coming at me, that question.

To leave had been selfish and to return could be too.

That's all I thought about day after hot summer day, baking in my crumbling studio apartment, a plastic fan blowing hot air in my face, enduring those long, repeating hours until the evening when I had to go to work.

And then the weather got a little cooler. September came.

The drop in temperature released me from total paralysis. I decided not to seek them out. Not yet at any rate.

I'd been away—either at war or abroad or in jail, even I wasn't entirely sure how to say it—and needed to come at them not as a ragged needy soul or even a pitiful apologetic one. I needed to stand on my own two feet. For my own sake as well as theirs, because in case of their rejection, which was a good possibility, I would need to be able to survive.

The first thing I did was clean my apartment. I'd let the place go and it had entered a moderate slovenliness. There was a meditative aspect to it. I sweated as I scrubbed at stubborn stains and crusts. My arms grew tired. I gagged on ammonia fumes. And even after the initial sally, a quickly fading sense of accomplishment would soon be replaced by each progressive hour's encroaching dust and scatter. But the act and symbol of discipline was a necessary foundation, and it also gave the day a regular chore that anchored it. And, somewhat ironically, it was the putting of my room in order that allowed me to leave it.

Cooking, too. Before, I'd lived on cereal and cheap takeout. But now I began making my own food, simple meals of rice or soup or beans or eggs. Slowly these meals evolved, incrementally, found a hidden basic balance. And so I walked to the store and the greengrocer, and I saw others more and glimpsed how they were and lived.

I saw others but I didn't yet feel seen. I was sexless background, a self-regulating machine that its creator had abandoned.

For the experience, I invite you to participate in city ghostness. It's an odd sensation that quickly becomes almost comfortable, almost second nature. Now human exchange has been reduced to transaction. That's what makes the ghosting possible. We even prefer it, at first. It's less energy to simply watch the numbers go up or down than try to confront a person's expression. And we don't realize until it's done that we've disappeared, gone invisible beside the transaction. We uncloak when we need to, I suppose, for touch, for anger or love. But if you have no reason or opportunity to, then you can live for quite a long time as a ghost, as an unseen agent in the market, softly padding to the void. Try it. It's little more than a loosening up, a letting go.

I'd test it out quite literally. I'd go to the busiest plaza, the most packed rooms, the jammed streets. And I'd stand just to the side, next to the thoroughfare or just against the jostle of bar bodies in Brownian motion. And the world would revolve around me, even, it felt, flow through me, and neither it nor I would sense it. We'd pass by each other untouched.

Ms. Mistleto stopped talking. Suddenly I felt the effects of the muscle paralyzer beginning to wear off. I realized I could move and quickly pulled out my raygun and scrambled to standing. Ms. Mistleto was already off at a sprint.

Still woozy from the drug, I stumbled after her. She ran onto the bridge and was dashing across it, about to escape to the other side. I aimed and fired my raygun; however, to my chagrin, at just the last second, Mistleto turned and took a dive into the Neretva River below. My blast obliterated the bridge, of course, but even after hours of combing through all the debris we could find no sign of her.

Meanwhile

"What do you think is better," Muriel asked us, "a methodical and consistent learning that tries for as complete as possible a coverage or, choice number two, a wandering study where progress is done by instinct and influenced by mood and present circumstance?"

"Ideally," said Dave, "one starts with the first and goes later, after some mastery, with the second."

I said, "The problem with the former is it's schematic and risks dogmatism and lifelessness, while the problem with the latter is it's potentially undisciplined and courts chaos."

"Stop beating about the bush," Muriel said. "What'll it be?"

"Court chaos," Dave said. And I nodded.

And so Muriel then cut the bright blue wire on the console. Fortunately for us this stopped the countdown to the lethal explosion and the city was saved.

I Wanted to Be Somebody

Long after I'd found out he was dead, for a period of about five to six months, Vu would visit me in my dreams. My wife was no longer in the picture. I lived with my son in a shabby two-bedroom. And then, it seemed a very short time later, my son graduated high school and moved out, and I was again alone.

(The problem with parasitism as method is it is barely distinguishable from invisibility, which itself is synonymous for living dead. I've no solution to this but offer that tracelessness in some religions is an attribute of the highest attainment.)

It was in the few months immediately after my son left home that I began dreaming about Vu. The two had somehow become intertwined in my mind.

The dream would always start in the same way, and at first it would seem to have nothing at all to do with Vu. It was instead a memory of my son. In my dream he's about four or five. Our elderly neighbor had had a stroke. I'm standing with my son on the sidewalk, and we're listening to the ambulance's powerful idling engine. And then, after the paramedics had loaded a pale Mrs. Falleagson into it, we watched its red and white lights as it drove away.

Going up the stairs to the apartment, he had asked, "What does *dead* mean?" It means you're fucked forever, I didn't say. And then I told him one of a variety of softened lies—to be honest, I don't even remember which. I only remember something in his voice when he'd asked the question.

And in my dream, which I'm suddenly aware is a memory, I struggle to see his childhood face. But the face I thought I saw so clearly now becomes strangely blocked as I try to observe it. He's either turned away, or I'm forced to, or my eyes suddenly water, or he's silent and we're both only looking out a window to the empty road where the ambulance once was.

1. Almost like a relief map, oceanic drifts and mountains. Yellow seas, lost and dead civilizations.

In the dream's logic, the next thing that happens is that I'm walking up First Avenue in Manhattan among a thick crowd that extends, it seems, for miles. I'm walking next to Vu, who asks me the date.

I know it, because I've often thought about it. I tell him it's February 15, 2003. We are participating in the largest antiwar demonstration in human history. Millions of people around the world have taken to the streets to make the public statement that they oppose the imminent war, an opinion that in the coming weeks the U.S.

government chooses to utterly ignore. "There's a certain cynicism," Vu says, taking my hand as we ascend in dream flight, "in revisiting this moment." We rise like drones and hover twenty feet above the massive crowd and begin gliding slowly through the skyscraper-made canyons. "I admit not only that," Vu continues, "but also that your son will helplessly return to the void from which he was snatched. Both of which are admissions that help nobody."

2. A constant yet static modulation between abstraction and landscape. An ice palace surrounded by sick fish during a blood-red sunset.

Then Vu says, "In L.A. I was taking classes at night and working as an art mover in the daytime." (While he is talking we fly to opposite positions in the sky and, like anime characters, begin conjuring energy bursts with our hands and hurling them at each other.) Vu says, "We'd move pieces from warehouse to gallery, or from gallery to warehouse, or from the gallery to some rich dude's mansion. We'd haul and install. It was low pay and backbreaking work, but I liked it because a lot of the time it involved just sitting in the truck and, because the guy I worked with was thankfully a quiet type, this gave me plenty of space and time to think."

3. White demons (or angels), blurred by speed, converging on a corpse. Or maybe just a fire in black and white.

Vu continued: I wanted to be somebody, but I couldn't figure out what that meant. It seemed important to make a name for myself, to not be pushed around and a small fry for the rest of my life, maybe even to push someone *else* around for a change. I wasn't sure.

But the only thing I was doing was painting. And even though part of me had aspirations there, I couldn't believe they were realistic.

I painted at night, after classes and work, trying to tell myself something. At the time I wasn't sure what, but now it seems terribly clear. I was telling myself that I was angry. And that I felt hopeless. And all I could do, it seemed to me then, was make soundless, impotent flags out of this fact and throw them off into dark deep space. I did this canvas after canvas, bad painting after bad painting, each work blunted with stupid, undeveloped rage. And then, each night, after I'd finished mangling some surface with paint, spent and tense, I'd jerk off and try to sleep.

4. A blown-up detail of a child's cartoon of flying purple ponies, just the mane.

At some point during this time I started hearing about this painter, Sonny Rhee. Friends said she was amazing, and so I decided to see for myself. I went and saw one of her paintings at an exhibit at the Hammer. It made me go out of my mind, it was so good.

But I kept doubting my enthusiasm. I'd go back to

look at it, kept getting blown away. My feelings would alternate between envy and admiration. But then I'd doubt myself again, think I was buying into someone else's sophisticated bullshit again—so ubiquitous and insidious and clever, these internalizations of someone else's bullshit.

And because I was unwilling to be so duped yet again, I'd go back to see the painting over and over.

5. Everything but the pine tree forest.

Sonny's reputation as a painter was rising, but the reason people knew her name and were talking about her was because she had an eccentric—some would say religious, others would say self-defeating—sense of business. Sonny allowed only twelve of her paintings to exist at any one time. Simultaneously she painted a new picture every month. What this meant was that when she finished a new painting, she would burn her oldest one.

It was an interesting process. Admirable and risky. But what made it even more diabolical was that she wouldn't sell any individual painting. You couldn't purchase a *single* Sonny Rhee painting. The artist demanded that any buyer purchase all twelve of her paintings. What's more, and this was the clincher, you weren't buying twelve paintings but only her twelve *most recent* paintings. The purchaser of these works had to sign a contract that obligated them to return, in order for Sonny to destroy it, her oldest painting in exchange for her newest work.

At first people were interested, intrigued, but the risks outweighed any curiosity. What if there was a decline in the work? What if you wanted a de Kooning *Excavation* and wound up with some Alzheimer goofs? Or maybe she'd paint a dozen middle fingers. People knew Sonny had a wicked sense of humor. Some nonetheless started to become interested. Her paintings were being praised to the skies, and her business demands were conceptually provocative. The sharks began circling. But then she raised the price of the contract. First a million dollars, then twelve million, then fifty.

    6. Crumbled erosion remnants and a black star to the upper left. Bright reborn white bottom right. In the middle: yellow ruins or a finished plate of runny eggs.

One day we were delivering and installing a huge painting. It was a Hirst or something similar, i.e., vile expensive bullshit. But we also knew that this one sale, and the few like it, were what in large part paid our wages, so we—my partner was an older guy named Sid—had pushed those kinds of thoughts, the bigger-picture thoughts, way down, at least as long as we were in the rich people's houses, and did our best to be invisible and friendly and get the job over with and done.

On that day when we arrive a man with some ambiguous eurozone accent says to us, *We're going to put this in the office*, and he leads us to a large sun-filled room. We then spend the better part of an hour installing this massive painting of primary-colored dots, which might as well have been dogs playing poker, over some banker's desk.

After we've finished, the man returns to assess its effect. Over his face breaks what can only be called an astoundingly self-satisfied and cartoonishly evil grin. He catches me looking at him and at first doesn't say anything, just gives me a conspiratorial wink. This was Neil.

We became friends, not great friends, but he was nonetheless a pivotal person in my life, because of two things. First, he represented a philosophy of parasitism that I came to respect but eventually had to reject. And second, he introduced me to Sonny.

His job, which he'd freely admit was sordid and neck deep in hypocrisy, was working for one of the better-known galleries in L.A. He was basically employed to buy art to complement the interior design of rich people's homes. Until I met Neil, I'd never known what people meant when they said of someone that they had "beautiful manners." Though he'd grown up the only son of a divorced civil servant in Cologne, he'd been a brilliant student and ended up at ETH Zurich and then had gotten a Ph.D. in art history from Berkeley. While he was a good negotiator, was extremely smart, and had mastered a kind of anthropological study—that is, he had absorbed and could mimic, signal, and manipulate the habits, vocabulary, and fashions of the ultrarich—what truly made him excellent at his job was that he was thin and tall and looked exquisite in a suit.

One day, after I tell him about the painting that I've spent hours gazing at, he tells me not only does he know Sonny Rhee but he's on decent terms with her. In fact, he's on such good terms that he gets me an invitation to a monthly dinner party at Rhee's place.

7. What Icarus saw, drowning.

It was a strangely intimate but subdued dinner. There were about ten of us. Rhee didn't talk much. Neil and a couple other wits dominated the conversation, which the rest of us, I think, were both annoyed by and grateful for. Logs were burning in the fireplace, and next to it, looking like the ready kindling it was, lay the painting. While I tried to examine it, it was too difficult to really see it in the middle of the party.

Someone served dinner and poured wine. Sonny then stood and picked up the painting and set it gently into the fire. I gasped but everyone else took it in stride. We lifted our glasses. It seemed Sonny gave me a kind, sad smile, but maybe it was for everyone. We toasted the burning painting and then began to eat. The flue was in good order and well maintained. We barely could smell the acrid scent from the burning oils.

8. Five heavy chairs in a room around a table in a field a great distance away in the back middle of the frame. Almost obscured.

I was hired as Sonny's assistant. I more or less begged her for the job, and Neil put in a good word for me. I dropped out of school and quit the art-moving gig.

One afternoon I asked her, Why just twelve?

Hm?

Why just twelve paintings?

She stopped and looked at me. Then she said, Because of Tehching Hsieh.

Who's that?

She pulled down a large coffee table book called *Out of Now*.

9. Magnified brain scans of people watching glamorized photos of death in war.

"He was born in Taiwan," Sonny said. "To get here he got a job as a seaman on an oil tanker, and then he jumped ship and lived in the U.S. illegally for many years. In the late '70s and early '80s he made six important performance works. No one really knew who he was. He was kind of a whisper; people talked about him, but he had barely an audience to speak of. His performances would last one year. The year is an important measurement of time for humans, he says, because it's the largest single unit of time that occurs naturally. He calls his artwork just acts of wasting time, which is all, he says, we ever do.

"His first one-year performance," Sonny continued,

flipping through the book to show me, "began in 1978. For a year he lived in a wooden cage and did nothing. He forbid himself to talk, read, or write. A friend brought him food and took away his waste." As she flipped through the pages of the book I saw a young man through cage bars, lying on a bed. "His second one-year performance was probably, I think, his toughest, at least physically. It's called *Time Clock Piece,* and while the former project had him confined by space, this confined him also by time. He punched in to a time clock in his apartment once every hour for a year. He therefore couldn't sleep for more than an hour or go very far from his apartment."

I flipped through pages of the book all showing film stills of a man next to a time clock. In the beginning his head was shaven, but as I turned the pages I saw his hair grow longer, finally coming down to his shoulders.

"He photographed himself at each punch-in and put together a film, which proceeds at a rate of twenty-four frames per second, so when you see this all put together, every second represents one day."

"What happened to him?" I asked.

"His fifth and sixth projects were different and are about *not* making art, or about making art and becoming invisible. In his last work he vows to make art but not to show it publicly for thirteen years. And he does this. At the end of this span, which coincides with his forty-ninth birthday, on December 31, 1999, all Tehching Hsieh reports about his trial is: *I kept myself alive.* And since then, he says he hasn't made any art.

"Tehching Hsieh," Sonny concludes, "gave me an understanding about time and patience. But what he really gave me, the most important thing, was something else. He gave me a kind of realism about protest art. Tehching Hsieh says, *I don't think that art can change the world. But at least art can help us to unveil life.*"

10. Scenes from a romance.

In the end I did something to piss Sonny off and eventually lost the job. She had a strict policy of not allowing anyone to photograph her work. Of course I photographed it as much as possible.

She caught me and said she was going to fire me, but as I was pleading my apology, she suddenly snapped her fingers, smiled, and said she'd thought of a suitable punishment. She was going to give me a job. I was to write her catalog. For each of her paintings I was allowed to write a very brief description. There would be no images in the catalog, so my words would be the only sanctioned remains of her work.

11. Outer space.

She was right about it as a punishment. It was a merciful but horrible purgatory to have the weight of that meaningful and yet meaningless responsibility. I knew she'd use my text, too.

Writing was never my strength, and I sweated hours

over those dozen descriptions. I also knew it was a joke at my expense, an impossible and absurd job she'd given me, or maybe a lesson. So, after several weeks, I allowed the futility of it to overtake me. I trashed everything I'd written, scribbled down the first things that came to my head, and, early the next day, I gave these to her.

She read them and laughed. She said, "Good job."

And then she fired me anyway, saying I was too young to be wasting any more time with her.

I was devastated but part of me knew she was right. There wasn't anything there left for me. After Sonny fired me I gave up painting and all of that completely. I decided instead to get rich, that it was the only sensible but senseless thing to do. It would be—for a moment I told myself this—a project similar to Sonny's paintings: dazzling and pointless and defiant.

I moved to New York and thought that after I made my millions I'd become Sonny's patron. I held on to that intention for a while, too, but then, after some time, not that long really, I gave up on this as well.

12. Beautiful world.

Speaking of cyborgs, dear. Does this augmentation make me look vestigial? Let's be real, bipeds and germs, today's puzzler: Who amongst us will opt out? Click poof to become forgotten click acquiesce to rising tide fallacy.

Special special bonus round: From where springs hope eternal?

Yours too sincerely,

From *Inspector Mush Tate and the Case of the Missing Daughter*

I came to in a cold, dark room. There was a lump on my head where one of Car's goons had polished his boots. My right wrist was tender from that wicked ju-jitsu mojo, but otherwise I felt sparkly.

In the distance I used a dim fuzzy line of light to orient myself to the land of the living. I must have still been off, however, because each time I tried to get up, the ground twirled and attached itself to my right biceps.

I crawled over the cement floor, feeling my way through the filth and wet and staying focused on that feeble glow. It seemed very far away. When I got close enough I saw it outlined the bottom of a boarded-up door. I was better by then and a little angry. For a bit of catharsis I kicked at the wood. Each hit rattled me to the spine, but on the thirteenth I heard a crack.

I got through to a long hallway. There was barely any light, just a single sulfur-colored bulb every forty yards. I made my way as fast as I could.

The corridor seemed to go on and on. The building was windowless, dank, subterranean. After a couple of hours I pushed through a set of emergency doors to an empty parking lot nestled under a lace of highway. It was night and there was the ocean sound of cars. I collapsed to the ground to catch my breath. It occurred to me that I should have asked the dad for more than my standard retainer.

Two weeks earlier a respectable-looking guy in his sixties—a middle-management type—had come into my office with the missing-daughter case. These were bread-and-butter jobs. Two thirds turned up a spoiled child shacked up with a boyfriend on an extended Molly vacation; however, this one seemed a more interesting variety, mostly because I knew the daughter. Not personally but by reputation. Eula Thomas was a poet and her first book had gotten some attention. It was titled *You're All Assholes Now Go Away*. A second book was about to be published. I'd preordered it. It was called *I Prefer Not to AND I Don't Want to Go Crazy*. I asked the dad a few questions and told him I'd be in touch.

Now I was icing the love taps Boss Car's pals had lain on me, wondering how she knew I'd bugged the judge's office. There was only one way. She must have bugged it first. Of course! That's how she knew all the details about the trial . . .

But I had to stop thinking of Car, even though I knew

I was getting close, because just then I received a message from my Asian sidekick, Guan Xi, who was tailing the missing girl's only known friend.

This was a woman named Lucy Drummond. Guan Xi said Lucy was on the move. Because she was my only real lead in the case, despite feeling like a crushed juice box, I had to jump.

As I turned the corner on Lucy Drummond's block I saw her coming down the building's steps. She was lugging a large, heavy suitcase. I didn't have time to step back, and so she saw me.

She dropped the suitcase, which fell down the stairs with three kettledrum thuds, and then she took off in the opposite direction at a dead sprint.

I ran after her, giving, as I passed it, a longing glance at the abandoned luggage.

Lucy ran straight across a broad avenue against traffic. An alert driver slammed on his brakes while a less alert one slammed into him. A bus swerved, nearly toppled over but didn't, and crashed back to the ground with the side-to-side sway of an elephant's ass. I slid over the hood of one car but had to go around the bus. I was losing her.

When I made it past the avenue I saw her dash into the open-air bazaar.

We both were slowed by the crowded aisles. I stumbled through the throng. A narrow opening cleared for her, and Lucy began running. I had to shove a fruit seller, whose wares, I'm sorry to say, spilled.

She got through the bazaar and crossed the street, where she ran into a restaurant. I went in just seconds after her but she was nowhere in sight. I gave a panicked look to a waiter, who pointed toward the kitchen. I banged through the set of saloon doors just in time to see her slide past the dishwasher and down some stairs.

A big guy, maybe the head cook, stepped in my way, saying, "What the fuck! You can't—" and I sucker-punched him in his throat. The rest of the kitchen staff started coming after me but didn't follow me down the stairs.

It seemed all the basements on that block were connected. I chased Lucy through narrowing halls and up another flight of stairs. She seemed to know where she was going.

As I was chasing her I thought to myself, "Whatever happened to *my* dreams of writing poetry? I guess I lacked the talent and the guts. I barely even read it anymore. Just as well, I guess. I've found my niche. Not everyone can be a private eye . . ." But at that moment Lucy pushed over a huge shelf full of paint cans. The shelf toppled toward me and I lost my train of thought as I evaded the tumbling metal and danced around the cans. "Wait!" I yelled, "I just want to talk!"

She ran down one hallway after another and then up

some stairs. She ran all the way up to the roof, and when I finally made it to the top, I'd lost her. She may have scrambled down a fire escape or sprouted wings but in any case she was gone. I swore and made my way back to the street.

I was surprised to see no one had taken Lucy's suitcase, but there it was, as we'd left it, wrong end down and aslant on the sidewalk. It almost looked like a guy was guarding it, but he seemed to just be killing time, because he walked off when I approached.

Looking through the suitcase and finding only clothes and knickknacks, I thought I'd come up entirely empty-handed, but then tucked into one side pocket I found something: a single ticket for a balcony seat to a concert that evening by a pianist named Emil Charbonneau.

I went home, scrubbed behind my ears, and put on my one fancy dress. I didn't know what I expected to find at the concert hall, but I knew that it was the only clue I had left. I got there about half an hour early and an usher led me with exaggerated regard to my designated balcony, which had only two seats.

I sat in one and studied the hall over my program. I recognized no one, and eventually the lights went out. Emil Charbonneau came on stage and began to play. The program told me it was Ravel's *Miroirs*. I was impressed, moved, and a little fidgety. Nothing seemed to be happening, and I concluded that whatever reason Lucy had for coming to this concert tonight must have changed. The music stopped and the audience applauded enthusiastically. We were in intermission.

I was wondering how I was going to break the news to Eula's father that I'd lost the trail, when the balcony door opened and Emil Charbonneau himself walked in and sat next to me.

"Lucy's safe," he said. "She ran because she thought you worked for Boss Car."

"What? Why—"

"You don't understand. Car's been manipulating all of us from the beginning. You think you're working on how she's shaking down Judge Shinohara, but that's just the tip of the arms deal. There's no end to the lengths Car will go to. She created an entire literary foundation just to give out fake awards so she could get her clutches on my sister. She gave Eula a huge sum, which she said was in honor of her poetry, but then insidiously began asking her for favors: attending particular parties, endorsing products in the lines of her poems, and using her celebrity to get certain politicians elected. Eula was horrified when she figured it out, but by then Boss Car had something—I don't know what—on her."

"So you're Sheldon," I said.

"Yes. Emil Charbonneau is just a stage name. My sister and I are Eula and Sheldon Thomas of Miljear, now of Ossining, New York. We are twins. And orphans. Our parents died when we were young. I hired you through a proxy. I didn't know then if I could trust you."

"And now?"

"I'm still not sure, Ms. Tate, but you're fairly talented at taking a beating. And, frankly, that's compelling me."

"I'm blushing."

"My sister really is missing, Tate. I'm not entirely sure why . . ."

And then Emil Charbonneau, also known as Sheldon Thomas—and also known, I was soon to find out, in certain other circles as Prince Surdenk Tomstita—said, "You see, Ms. Tate, Eula and I didn't always live in Ossining. We were born and spent our childhoods on the island nation of Miljear. As you may or may not know, the people of Miljear have over millennia developed, and used as a staple of their diet, an ancient grain called 'milj' (in fact, *Miljear* simply translates to 'people of the milj'). The grain has remarkable nutritional content, provides a subtle and nonaddictive but very pleasant narcotic effect, can be described as tasting like apples baked with brown sugar, and what's more is a complete protein providing all the essential amino acids in a nonanimal food source.

"At some point anthropologists, coming under the guise of philanthropic research but actually on the payroll of a multinational's R&D department, came and quote *discovered* milj. It soon became a global dietary sensation. Not only vegetarians but health-conscious people of all stripes and nationalities wanted to eat milj along with their tofu, chia, kale, and hijiki. They developed milj burgers and milj pasta. This led to a great economic boom time in Miljear. My parents Glidk and Mjeespquatch-roont Tomstita (we changed our last name when we im-migrated) were then king and queen. It was a tumultuous time of transformation when Miljear went from being a poor agrarian nation to an economic tiger.

"The milj production could barely keep up with de-mand, but this only drove prices higher. Despite warn-ings of soil exhaustion, farmers no longer diversified their crops and planted only milj. The irony, not lost on Mil-jeari, was that everyone was now rich—however, even so, no one could afford to eat milj. It had become too precious and was hoarded and eaten now only on feast days. Eventually, with what I believe were the best of in-tentions to safeguard Miljear's future, my parents sold the genetic reproductive rights of the milj seed to a corpora-tion in exchange for their funding of a massive develop-ment plan that sought to bring Miljear into the modern era. However, when news of this agreement became pub-lic, Miljeari everywhere felt betrayed. Headlines blared that the very soul of the country had been commodi-fied and sold. Riots broke out and my parents were dragged through the streets and executed. The irony, of course, is that no one eats milj now. It was simply a fad. People have moved on to quinoa and açai berries. When demand col-lapsed the economy was thrown into chaos.

"But all that is in the history books and well known.

What is harder to explain, perhaps, is what it was like to grow up during this time and the impact it had on myself and, of course also, on my sister."

The lights in the concert hall suddenly blinked, signaling that the intermission was almost over. "I've run out of time and I have to go," said Sheldon, and he slipped me a piece of paper. "Go here now. This is where Lucy is. She's waiting for you." He then shook my hand rather seriously and turned and left the balcony.

As instructed, I left to go find Lucy. She was staying at a hotel in the financial district. When I got there I noticed her room door was ajar and I heard muffled noises and the sounds of a struggle.

Entering, I saw two of Boss Car's goons were holding Lucy hostage. I used my four-inch heels to incapacitate one and then tasered the other. I grabbed Lucy's hand and we ran as the goons came to and gave chase. With some pushiness I commandeered a motorcycle, which we weaved at high acceleration through night streets. The goons were hot on our tail in a muscular SUV. At the docks on the East River we jumped off the bike. I hotwired a speedboat and we churned and then powered through the water. The goons called in backup and soon a helicopter was hovering over us taking potshots. I told Lucy to take the speedboat's wheel and then, fashioning a tether from our jackets and a small anchor I'd found, managed to climb onto the helicopter above us. I feinted right and then quickly left, causing one goon to fall into the river below. Then I used an old muay thai move to knock the pilot unconscious. Taking over the helicopter, I called out to Lucy to dock nearby, and then used the helicopter to take us to a very nice sushi restaurant I happened to like in Midtown. After we were seated I told Lucy what Sheldon had recounted. She said:

"Sheldon wants to understand why Eula's decided to disappear but he just can't. He wants to think of Eula as a victim. Eula's not that kind of victim. She's a different kind of victim. The same we all are. Sheldon is the apologist, the mouse, a parasite. The get-along-to-get-along type. Smart, survivalist, but fundamentally soft and selfish.

"Eula's different. She wants to do something, to break free, to be pure if only briefly and even if requiring sacrifice. She's the energy for it. She's a poet.

"Our plan is twofold. Take revenge on Boss Car and then get the fuck out of Dodge. The second's the priority—to get out—but the first would be sweet.

"How about you, Ms. Mush Tate? Are you down? Think you're much? Know you're living? We plan on taking the struggle to the source. That's right. You're in convo with separatists, off-the-gridders, R-slash-evolutionaries. What's-a-matter? You ain't gonna cry on me now, are you, Tate? After you clobbered all those meanies for me?

"See, I drew them in to watch you work, to study your

technique, so I could measure the right shoe size for your particular Achilles' heel, get me? The paranoid making you paranoid yet?

"Someone said we can weaponize our invisibility, our outcast status, by converting it into anonymity. We may do that. The point is we're out of here. It's the only escape. The rest is lying to yourself. That's what we've decided. And we're tough. We can do it. But we have to keep it lean and mean. Just us and on the run and slash and burn.

"*Is* there another way? Maybe there's not even this way. The culpability and embeddedness so tight and inextricable.

"We're going to make a perfect sand painting, a masterpiece ice sculpture—and then suicide-pact our way into history I mean oblivion."

Then Lucy stood up.

I'd underestimated her. She'd spotted me long ago and had figured out how to make me sit when she said sit. All of a sudden I thought, Was she just another underling of Boss Car in some matryoshka-doll strategy to get me off the scent or, worse, was this all just an elaborate and slow assassination? Were all these action-scene terms just another disguise with which the state entrapped me? What was the state? Was *I* the state? My head was a muddle. Maybe Lucy had put something in my drink. The only thing clear at all was that Lucy and I were about to start a fierce hand-to-hand battle that would absolutely wreck the carefully designed mannerisms of the restrained sushi restaurant.

I stood up and yelled, "En garde!"

In an Alternative Universe

In an alternative universe I had dinner with
Vu and Frank's sister. Champagne flutes.
A cheese course. After years of activism she
said she wasn't bitter. Not anymore. Sad
maybe. But perhaps that's what, underneath
the rest, she'd said, the universe was like.
Vu was rich from an invention. Somehow
they'd met and married. I was either a one-
time bomber who'd gone underground but
who now wanted to come in from the cold,
so to speak, or a bachelor wilting away in
upper management. Probably both. An extended layover. By this time we were practically strangers. I mean I'd just flown in.
They seemed glamorous but post-prime. I
think it was on the first floor of a hotel Vu
knew about in old downtown. After that
night we never saw each other again. An un-
spoken pact I've often regretted.

True Death Speaks

On the afternoon of March 28, 2015, the four of us—Dave, Muriel, Frank, and me—stumbled into the cool air outside the Zinc Bar. We stumbled and looked dazed not because we were drunk but because we'd just borne witness to an incredible performance.

At an open mic, a famous filmmaker and poet, then ninety-two, whom we thought that day looked older and more frail than any of the other times we'd caught a glimpse of him around town at this or that art show or this or that screening or this or that dive bar or, surprisingly rarely, inside the beautifully semidilapidated, municipally inflected film theater and archive he'd created, had taken to the stage and read, had *performed*, a simply conceived narrative about his relationship with a typewriter. It was gradually made evident that it was as simple perhaps as time. And somehow it absorbed such sweet tragedy that we wept at its telling. His frailty perhaps even lent itself to, perhaps purposefully was used in, this devastating performance, so that it felt less like a literary act than perhaps a last testament, in which the man with the miraculous life spanning continents and a century, during which he'd conversed and had been in many cases friends with the great artists of his time, admitted knowing nothing, having no meaning to speak of, claimed to be depthless and thoughtless, and maintained if anything that he, if forced, could only testify to pitiable sorrows known and caused by the gulf between beings. He said this all lightly, at first, and only at the end, reluctantly, did he reveal, behind the seemingly entire, impish mirth, a wide, dark ocean of implacable sorrow.

We stood outside the bar and took in the afternoon air.

"That was pretty good." Muriel said.

"Yeah," said Frank.

Dave said, "Let's go get lemonades and sit on a bench." We went into a place.

In line for our drinks, Muriel said, "I guess what we just saw was death, death speaking."

"But not its threat," Frank said, "not the grim reaper speaking, which is what people usually mean when, if ever, they talk about death speaking."

"No, you're right," Muriel said. "This time it was true death we heard—oblivion, void, the absolute—and the beauty of the experience was rooted in our sadness in acknowledging living within it. That's what True Death would say. Not *I'm coming for you* but *You always dwell within me.*"

Our conversation paused at that moment because on a television monitor in the coffee shop was what appeared to be scenes from a game show, perhaps a Japanese one, and we all noticed it for the first time. It was some kind of brutal yet cartoonish show where contestants in brightly colored and strangely appendaged costumes took part in diabolically difficult races, the courses of which had all manner of humiliating nets and walls and mud pits and stumbling blocks and other devices to frustrate the contestants' progress. Muriel, Dave, Frank, and I were instantly fascinated and involuntarily forgot our previous conversation and stopped talking to gawk.

On the monitor we saw a crowd of contestants running toward a wall,

which it looked initially like they would have to scale.

However, as they approached it we saw on the wall, spaced evenly apart, eight rectangular outlines that looked like doorways.

Each "doorway" was covered over with bright blue paper.

However, only one of the eight was an actual opening.

Through this opening, a contestant could crash through the bright paper and pass through the wall.

The other "doorways" were actually decoys, and for these the bright paper hid only solid wood.

We figured this out soon enough—simultaneously with the contestants, it seemed—as the horde of them appeared to scream and run at the wall.

One lucky person was able to break through the paper to the other side.

Most of the others bounced painfully back as they were repulsed by the fake doorways.

(The contestants wore helmets, were in neon-green body suits, and had on their backs puffy pink wings.)

The fallen quickly stood up; some shook their heads as if to throw off any injury or to reorient themselves.

All then bellowed again (it appeared this way, the sound was off) and ran after the first who had successfully chanced upon the opening.

We saw that what awaited them, about thirty yards past the first wall, was yet another wall, again with seven ficti-tious openings and one real one.

This challenge repeated itself several more times with in-creasing additions and impediments.

For example, before one wall contestants had to hurry over a slippery rail-thin beam floating over moats of excre-ment, or

before another, pendulums of huge, heavy, foam-covered hammers swung perpendicular to the contestants' path, or

before reaching yet another wall, strong fat men skimpily dressed as fairies tried to tackle the contestants and pin them to the ground,

et cetera.

Frank, Muriel, Dave, and I were utterly
captivated and frozen like

statues for ten minutes and broke free only when the
show went to commercial, at which point we found lids
for our drinks and left the shop.

Dave spoke first when we were outside and said, "That
was amazing."

"Yeah," said Frank.

Muriel said, "Have you seen the show where audience members vote on which pregnant teenaged contestant has the mother with the worst botched cosmetic
surgery?"

We continued our walk to the park. Our lemonades
were delicious, not too tart but not too sweet. The sun
had come out, and it felt all of a sudden like spring. It felt
really great.

"Have you found a place to take your breaks at work?"
asked Dave of Muriel after a few minutes.

"Yes," she said, "but I'm afraid it's an uninspired if
conniving solution. I go to Burger King. Or I go to Mc-
Donald's. Or I go to Wendy's. I can always get a seat and
the prices are affordable.

"The only problem, however," she continued, "is the
food. It's too tasty. This mass-produced, environmentally
corrosive food is, is . . . It's so delicious! At least it doesn't
take long to think of it that way. So I've been gaining

weight and risking hypertension and diabetes by consuming bacon and fried potatoes and hormone-loaded red meat several times a week. I always only mean to get a cup of coffee but end up instead with a large cheeseburger loaded with salt and fat and a good-sized, occasionally supersized, companion order of French fries, which I will dip with temporary abandon into a wonderfully cute, pleated paper cup of ketchup.

"And to drink?" I asked.

"Usually a diet beverage."

"It's actually the same," said Frank, stating the obvious, as if Muriel wasn't aware, "as your digitized cafeteria. These types of places are a cousin to that technological development. Economies of unthinkably vast scale allow the production of cheap, unsubtle food that overrides your limbic system with heavy, carnal signals so as to hide its exact resemblance to slow-acting poison. And this so-called food is served to you by a member of an underclass practically invisible to you, untouchable by you, unspeakable *to* except perhaps to complain and unspeakable *of* except perhaps to yourself with subconscious and subvocalized disdain, and yet, almost needless to say, a person whose destiny could have been exchanged for your own but for capricious circumstance. And this meal, so-called, once placed on a tray for you to take to your seat, will be eaten within an almost indestructible yet disposable shelter composed of polyurethanes, petrochemicals, fiberglass, and the occasional piece of metal—restaurant castles, in other words, that rival geodesic domes in their modular, architectural ingeniousness."

"Everyone knows that," Muriel sighed. "But what can you do?" she added and then turned to watch a skateboarder riding past and successfully leaping a hydrant.

I said then, but this was met with silence only, "Maybe Muriel is right. I mean, since these temptations and short-cuts are unavoidable, impossible to outwit, maybe Muriel should use them to proceed with her own desires—at least those desires that she can maintain somehow as *her* desires, as somehow independent and free and not de-formed (a feat in itself) by these humiliations and degra-dations. And she should pursue these desires using these corrupt means as would a freeloading parasite. Why not? Take your breaks and do your sketches and read poetry chapbooks at Wendy's or Burger King or McDonald's, especially—and this surely could be a measurement of your will, at least an exercise of it—especially if you can mostly avoid the food and only have a coffee. Or," I con-cluded, "a diet soda, even."

No one spoke.

"Shit," said Frank suddenly. "I think I left my book at the bar."

"Do you want to go back?"

"Naah," he said after considering it, "I'll go back later."

Then, after another minute, Dave said, "Some Koreans, elderly, a gaggle of grandmas and grandpas, did just what you're doing, Muriel. They would use this McDonald's down the road from my apartment. At first it was three or four of them, but then slowly word started to spread and dozens of Korean senior citizens would habitually come and take the place over. They'd each buy just one cup of dollar coffee. Some would get there at five in the morning and stay past dark. You have to imagine coming in during the lunch rush and finding there a classroom of *halmeonis* and *harabeojis* talking the blues or gossiping or recounting what they saw on last night's soap opera installment; that is, raising a ruckus and having a grand old time. The franchise owner eventually got sick to death of this. He started calling the cops on the parasite geezers and kept having them thrown out. They'd just walk around the block and then come right back.

"Word of the conflict spread and even made the international news. (The press focused only on how the government should intervene—primarily to enable the capitalist enterprise to continue. They suggested free shuttle vans to senior centers.) The reaction of the public to the story varied. Some blamed the business owner, saying he should know better in this heavily Asian neighborhood than to disrespect the elderly, but many sided with the business and said the seniors were taking unfair advantage and should be ashamed. The seniors eventually conceded and dispersed or found other places or simply stayed at home and died.

"So the lesson here, Muriel, is that you have correctly found the locations to enact a strategy of parasitism; however, heed the warning, for if you become too noticeable a strain, too large or successful or seemingly independent, the host body will strike to destroy you, as is logical," Dave concluded, "to save itself."

At his condescending analysis we all reacted by staring ahead blank-faced.

In the ensuing quiet I formulated a thought, which I ended up not saying, because I was scared I'd end up embarrassed. The story I wanted to tell was a mix of titillation and tragedy, and I thought I would not be able to get across the proper sense of its tragedy, that it would be trumped by its cheaper infamy.

I wanted to say:

This might interest you, friends, since when hearing such stories your subtle and unsubtle markings as Orientals— once so-called—flash and flush like spilled blood sprayed with luminol.

I saw the photograph of him first, before I knew anything else about him.

It says a lot, this photograph, some of it lies.

But what says more is how much I love it, this photograph.

A black-and-white image. A man has on his head a beret with a pin for one of the very first pan-Asian-American political groups, and indeed the photo is from 1968. He is young and unsmiling, eyes hidden behind sunglasses. The man raises an almost mocking, but ready, fist.

In another photo the man holds a sign that reads YELLOW PERIL SUPPORTS BLACK POWER.

This is Richard Aoki, whose childhood was spent in captivity in the desert in Topaz, Utah, at a Japanese internment camp, and later in Oakland, California. He grew up to become a prominent figure in the protest movements of the '60s and '70s. A leader of the Third World Liberation Front, he helped to organize a pivotal 1969 strike at the University of California at Berkeley that demanded the establishment of a "Third World College" developed "by Third World faculty, by Third World students and Third World community." The result of this strike and a previous one at San Francisco State was the creation of an entirely new academic field, Ethnic Studies, and from it grew, along with several other disciplines, Asian-American Studies.

Aoki would also become the highest-ranking non-black member of the Black Panther Party for Self-Defense. A sensational yet true part of his legend was that he was an early provider of arms to Bobby Seale and Huey Newton. He brought them guns and trained the Panthers in their use.

After a long illness Aoki committed suicide in 2009. At the time of his death he'd achieved iconic status as a movement leader. However, shortly after, a journalist would publish a book about the FBI's assault on the student radicals of the era. In his research the journalist discovered evidence that Richard Aoki, at the time of the student strikes and also throughout his early involvement with the Panthers, was an informant for the FBI.

This revelation is explosive. Aoki is for many a principal character of the struggle and, for many Asian Americans at the time, a rare early example of someone who understood, and lived in solidarity with, African Americans and other people of color. His entire life was spent analyzing and discussing how power operated, how class structures were created and maintained, and how racism was inextricable with that operation and structure. Moreover, he applied this analysis in a fight for radical causes.

That this man was a snitch for the state was not only a seismic revelation, it was a heartbreaking one.

His friends and supporters maintained Aoki's innocence and claimed he was being framed. But the journalist persisted, and through the Freedom of Information Act obtained and released more than two hundred pages of FBI documents, which, while heavily redacted, convincingly provided details of Aoki's informant activity.

(While his politics would change significantly, as a very young man Aoki served in the army and had strong anti-left convictions, largely due to a hatred of FDR, who had signed Executive Order 9066. An important detail—which lends itself to the argument that Aoki's informant career was a youthful error, albeit a massive and consequential one, but one he later transcended—is that when Aoki was initially recruited, it was to work against the Communist Party. Aoki often made the point that after FDR incarcerated Japanese citizens in concentration camps, the Communist Party fell in line and expelled Japanese Americans from its membership. Aoki's work for the FBI then was arguably triggered by a life-changing act of state racism and a resulting fiery and mis- and redirected rage.)

The analysis of race and power that became institutionally codified in the Ethnic Studies departments in California, and which has since spread to institutions nationally and worldwide, has had, to understate it, a great impact. In many ways this ongoing analysis and study is the intellectual engine driving today's continuing battle for justice and civil rights. This is so much the case that one can not only excuse the late Fred Ho's defense of his friend but even believe to be true his statement, "If Aoki was an agent, so what? He surely was a piss-poor one because what he contributed to the movement is enormously greater than anything he could have detracted or derailed."

Still, the long-held lie is devastating. Especially, for better or worse, to those wanting heroes.

And Aoki's story is haunting and important—I want to say to Frank and Muriel and Dave—also, maybe chiefly, because it is such an American story in that it tells the tale of a particular kind of passing. This particular passing is both a result of authenticity anxiety and its opposite—and similarly inextricable with social mobility. Aoki is a character buffeted and tossed by hurricanes of history—the internment camps, Panthers, Hoover—but one who nonetheless tries to be a person of conviction, even as those convictions adjust to turbulent circumstance. This utterly and helplessly American character: the secret and self-elected perpetual foreigner modulating between a double and triple identity, this willful imposter suffering from imposter syndrome.*

But I didn't say any of this to my friends.

And, after some time, one of us said, "It's actually impossible—did you know? I wikipedia'd it—for an algo-

---

*But then a voice said to me, "Don't be like that. There are heroes, imperfect but admirable. Grace Lee Boggs, Alex Hing, Fred Korematsu, Lee Lew-Lee, Larry Itliong, Philip Vera Cruz, Yuri Kochiyama, Liz Ouyang, Harvey Dong . . . Or how about Kiyoshi Kuromiya." "Who?" I said. "Kiyoshi Kuromiya. He was principled, subversive. He was like Nanquan Puyuan and the cat." "Who?" "Kuromiya was born in the internment camps, worked with SNCC in Alabama during Selma, was a close aide to MLK, a student of and collaborator with Buckminster Fuller, an early medical marijuana activist, was an early member of ACT UP and the Gay Liberation Front, created in the early '90s a newsgroup to collect and distribute (first by mail then via the internet) the latest news about HIV/AIDS to thousands of patients, and was a world-ranked Scrabble player to boot." "Never heard of him," I said, "and you know what else?" "What?" "If I haven't heard of him he's just that sad thing—" "What's that?" "A footnote in history." "Shut up and listen to this. When your guy Aoki was working with (or entrapping) the Third World Liberation Front, Kuromiya pulled off this stunt at the University of Pennsylvania. It's 1968, and the U.S. is using biological and chemical weapons on the Vietnamese. Napalm, Agent Orange. Leaflets start to circulate on campus saying that a group calling itself Americong is going to stage a demonstration: at noon they're going to use napalm to burn an innocent dog in front of the library. You can imagine the reaction. Two thousand people show up. Veterinarians and dog owners show up. The mayor announces that anyone who harms a dog is going to jail. It's later described as the largest anti-war demonstration in the school's history. Another leaflet starts being passed around among this well-meaning, liberal crowd. It says, 'Congratulations, you've saved the life of an innocent dog. How about the hundreds of thousands of Vietnamese that have been burned alive? What are you going to do about it?' Kiyoshi Kuromiya was the author of both pamphlets."

rithm, for a machine like our computers to, by themselves, generate a truly random order? We can create randomness ourselves easily. By flipping coins or rolling dice or otherwise. But a computer will always generate some kind of order, not true randomness. Order is in a computer's fundamental structure, its bottom layer. (Whatever is *our* foundational layer, we now know only that it is not order.) Most of the time fake randomness, the approximation or *appearance* of random order, is sufficient. However, in our cyborg world there are often times when true randomness is required. For these, the world currently uses machines called TRNGs, True Random Number Generators. Rather than from the too-clean, overly determined world of math, these machines use the world to create—from the photoelectric effect or quote atmospheric noise—strings of numbers that are in an actual random order. The machines have pseudorandomness; the world has actual randomness; and cyborgs have True Random Number Generators."

"Well, what I want to know," another one of us said, "is whether an internet search has a plot. There is an intense interaction and a development, a personality, and even a rising conflict and eventual resolution. But, really, I wonder. Does it?"

"Do we care," asked another, "about any of that? We're still simple narrative animals, that's the undergirding structure of *us*. It's still lizard brain underneath. Hunt, fuck, eat. Tell us something about that. Whisper what our lizard brains need to know. Tell us an old tale of desire and mystery."

"A few years ago," Dave said, "I was living in San Francisco and somewhat depressed. I'd lost my job as a web page designer and had to move in with my uncle, who was my only relative left and who ran, still runs, a dry-cleaning place there. He let me stay and gave me a little money for helping out, but he couldn't really give me much. I was confused because I had wanted to be a painter and that hadn't panned out but had thought I was able to live as an adult because I could design a web page. I knew this wasn't real work, or it didn't seem like real work, and it also didn't seem so difficult that anyone else couldn't do it—but somehow I kept finding paying jobs. But then something changed. The aesthetic changed and I wasn't hip anymore. And different parts of the job became automated. It was really a short time when that kind of work was viable, but it happened to be the only skill, if you could even call it that, that I had bothered to pick up. My mind was chaotic. I'd never really wanted a job in the first place. But now I guessed I did.

"Then one day a riot broke out.

"People had been fuming about the obscene billions that poured into the pockets of a certain few in the area, those who had been smart enough or well-positioned enough or lucky enough to be the first to market, those who had adapted and created technologies and so had started the first wave of cyborg culture. The whole world had joined in and adopted these new devices—those who could, and the others who were initially left out came along eventually—and so it seemed less like a collective preference for a certain type of product than a next evolutionary stage. The native people, the immigrants, the various rent boys and sex workers, the working poor, the deadbeat hippies, the sleepy original San Franciscans were rudely awakened and practically thrown out of bed.

"At first these alienated locals just muttered their complaints or vandalized or committed sporadic arson. But then one day someone, a group of people, snapped. It became more serious, focused.

"They started hijacking the Google buses and the Facebook buses and the Apple buses and the eBay buses— that is, the special corporate vehicles that shepherded the Content Strategists and Sales VPs and Analytics Managers and Interaction Engineers and Risk Analysts and Data Scientists, and all the other employees of the internet empires to their quote campuses in the South Bay. One person did it but then dozens followed suit. The first to do it had a gun and muscled his way onto a bus, kicked everyone off, and then led the cops on a televised high-speed chase through the Presidio before he ran the bus into a building and died. He was, however, instantly martyred, because the following week a coordinated bunch copycatted. They hijacked several buses, either kicking everyone off or keeping them hostage. Groups would take over a bus, empty it, and then set it on fire. One insane ex-hippie made all his hostages eat their phones.

"Since all was instantly made known via status updates and tweets and viral videos, from these few instances the city suddenly bloomed into riot.

"I was in my apartment following everything on my computer, growing more and more excited by what I was reading and seeing. It felt like an opening.

"To what, I wasn't sure. I'd been forced to take a job on the graveyard shift at a twenty-four-hour fast-food restaurant to augment the little allowance made at my uncle's dry cleaner. I was employed to pace from drive-through window to cash register with a huge headset on, saying into the night air upsell bids to lonely night owls. To deprived old men and women or to taxi drivers and office janitors going to or getting off the job, I'd ask, 'Would you like to make that a combo?'

"I was excited by the news of riot, but I had to go to work. So I reluctantly left my computer, put on my ugly uniform, and left the living room of my uncle's apartment. I passed fires and crowds and sirens and broken glass, not really understanding them and their relation to myself, wondering only if they'd be there later, if they'd impact my commute. Part of me was excited by the evident eruption but the rest of me couldn't believe that it had anything to do with me.

"But then at work, pacing in the quiet, harshly lit interior of the restaurant ('welcome to'), thinking about what I'd read ('will that be special, large') and seen ('or jumbo sized?'), I realized the oppressive order ('fries, tots, or rings?') that had ruled and contained ('and what kind of soda?') the more natural and real chaos in my own mind ('barbeque or sweet and') as well as the unjust order ('with bacon?') that seemed to deny and punish many ('limited-time offer') for the great material benefit of the few ('with cheese'), that this order might be collapsing ('that'll be eight seventy-five'). And so at that moment I took off my headset and walked off the job. I went looking for the fires and the mobs. They weren't hard to find. They were everywhere.

"I'd walked not too far when I came across the remnants of one of the hijacked buses.

"The bus had been driven hard into a cement barrier and its front was caved in and crushed. On one side of the bus someone had spray painted: *It is easier to imagine the end of the world than the end of capitalism*. On the other side the company's logo was written out in brightly colored, giant letters. I circled the bus several times and each time read first the graffitied phrase and then the company's name, and each time all the letters failed to make any sense. I didn't know who I was, and not for the first time I longed for the certainty others were so quick to display. The front of the bus was mangled—cracked plastic and bizarrely torqued metal—and around it was a nimbus of sprayed glass. The back, however, was pristine. I circled the bus, reading that phrase and the corporation's name, again and again and again.

"After some time, people started gathering around, maybe simply because I'd taken an interest. Or maybe, a sizable and notable piece of ruin, the bus had the draw of a beached whale.

"I kept circling and people continued to gather around my orbit. I was glad and awed to see the bus broken, but in my circling, I began to feel the bus wasn't yet beyond recovery, that it hadn't been destroyed quite *enough*. And so I started to pick at it. With two hands I strained at the cracked plastic, trying to pull back layers, anticipating the moments a piece would snap. I tore off several bits as if working on a scab. Then eventually I grabbed a nearby metal barricade, something thoughtlessly left by the police, and hurled it at an unbroken window. This activated the surrounding crowd.

"People appeared with bats and crowbars and two-by-fours. They took these and swung at the bus with all their might. The bus held up well, getting only pockmarks, puny injuries—but the crowd persisted, got angrier. And in the end, when our feeble blows couldn't inflict the needed amount of damage, we succumbed to unoriginality; that is, we set it on fire.

"After the flames were lit, the crowd quickly dispersed. It was as if this final act of arson was too heinous or too obvious, and it's true that soon the police did arrive. But I stood there for a few minutes, seeing the destruction but not satisfied with it, growing still more and more angry. I wanted something still bigger, more profound, to match my confusion and the sense of futility that had been growing and seemed to have consumed all my hope.

"Someone tapped me on the shoulder.

"I turned to see a black guy about my age, tall with a little roundness to him—maybe a tech kid, I thought when I saw his hip glasses. But then he said, 'That's nice what you did.'

"'I didn't do anything,' I said.

"'You started it. You did *that*,' he said. I shrugged.

"Then he said, 'Do you want a blow job?'

"'What?' I said.

"'I'll suck you off. Not for money. I mean. Just as a thank-you.'

"I smiled. 'That's okay.' And I added, 'Thanks.'

"'You'll like it,' he said. 'Don't worry. I *want* to do it.' He took my hand. I didn't pull away. All around us because of the rupture, because of the rioting, or just because of the very fact of violence, there'd been a growing charge in the air. Again, I felt some kind of opening. Though, again, an opening to what I wasn't sure. I heard the police sirens coming. He led me just a few blocks away and took me down a dark side street and there, behind a dumpster, he unzipped my pants and gave me an expert and gratifying blow job. I groaned and came.

"He stood up and faced me. Instinctively I felt for his cock through his jeans. He was hard. He smiled and quickly pulled it out for me and I began to jerk him off. He said, 'Do it this way,' and spat on my hand. I did as he said, gripping a little tighter and going a little faster until he, too, groaned and I saw a dribble of his semen on my hand.

"He gave me another smile. Together we walked out into the street. We headed back toward the burning bus.

"More and more police had arrived, were arriving, and this itself had attracted a new crowd. The growing throng was chanting and beginning to taunt the cops. We pushed our way up to the front. I wanted to see what had happened to the bus, but now there was a line of cops between us and it. Someone shoved us from the back and we were forced into the cops. Someone else threw a bottle. The police started pushing with their batons and then striking out with them. The crowd began retreating, but now the police were infuriated and started grabbing people as they could and beating them. Vans arrived, and they started handcuffing the beaten and herding them into these.

"Suddenly, from beside me, the man who had given me the blow job was grabbed by a cop. I saw him get hit viciously two times with a baton. He cried out and crumpled and then raised his head to look at me, to see what I had done and what I would do. I hadn't moved. I didn't say anything. As soon as he looked at me, I turned around and pushed my way back through the crowd, and then I walked away.

"After several nights and days of this, of wandering and fighting and running, after having survived without injury this riotous time, I came home and collapsed. And then the next morning or week, or maybe the next month or the next next one, I got up and started looking for a new job."

Dave stopped speaking.

The day had gotten colder and darker. After a few more minutes of walking, it occurred to each of us that it was a good time to part company, and, without having to say so, we all agreed.

However, before we did, as a continuation of a game that they sometimes played, Muriel gestured with only her eyes at a surveillance drone hovering a great distance above us, maybe thirty or forty feet. Dave deftly took out his slingshot and in one quick, subtle movement flung a stone that—ting!—struck the drone, making it stutter and fall halfway to the earth before it compensated and wobbled back up to its designated perch in the air.

I smiled at this feat. And then we took our leave. Frank decided to go back to the bar to see if he could find his book. Dave and Muriel went to catch the subway. And I, by allowing my atoms to disperse, appeared to dissolve quickly and quietly into the air.

Dear Cyborgs,

Cloud versus fog. Indra's net versus mirrored pirate servers. Worldwide web versus world. The internet of things versus a panopticon versus irreducible shame. Hacktivism versus feeds versus hunger strike. First-person shooter versus first-person shooter versus first-person shooter versus.

Now score yourself. One through seven is suicidal ideation, eight through twenty is dead man walking, twenty-one plus is immortal vegetative state.

Today's final puzzler: Don't give up!

Yours,

The Origin Story of Ms. Mistleto

I was working at a place called Zones, a comic-book shop in the East Village. While it had a mild suggestion at the time of urban chic, it was essentially no different from the dank, mismanaged store I'd gone to as a kid in rural Ohio.

(When I say *cyborgs*, of course I mean us.)

In fact, all the comic-book shops in the world are really just one essential place, and their entrances but doors to a single coincidence. That's why you always see there, no matter where you are, the same dreamy, awkward clientele.

For example, one day a tall, skinny man in a rumpled suit walked in. We saw each other and both shook our heads in disbelief. It was Vu.

———

(Some seem unaccepting of this transformation, and it indeed has been gradual. In a sense it began when the first simple machines were invented. But now, to deny the change requires a willful ignorance since, if you observe bodies clothed in steel flowing over highways, or how we've outsourced half our memory to these devices, these exobrains we carry around, and if you note how even our most intimate relationships occur remotely, at great distances from one another, if you see all this, well, it isn't such an original observation, dear cyborgs, to say that human and machine long ago merged inextricably.)

It had been about fifteen years since Vu and I had last seen each other.

He was wealthy now. He'd dropped out of school, but he'd been ambitious. He'd moved to New York and had talked his way into a stock-trading job with a false diploma and a faked transcript. This was discovered about three months into the job, but by then the bosses liked him and he was kept on. This happened during the early, unregulated days of momentum day trading, and Vu quickly made and lost and then made again several fortunes.

Every day, after the market closed, to clear out his mind and try to thin out the corrosive bursts of adrenaline that sugared his heart and brain each time a chart made an unexpected jag, Vu would walk the crepuscular but fulgent canyons of lower Manhattan trying to remind himself that he really didn't care what happened and that, for his own entertainment, he was playing an absurd game—not because he really believed this but because it helped him to think it.

On the night he walked into Zones he'd had a rather profitable day and was in a good mood. We were both immediately ecstatic to see each other. I think if it had happened in another, less surprising way, we might each have balked, both maybe (I certainly was) guilty and confused about why the once-tight friendship had so completely broken off. But the reason was probably the same reason we could start up so quickly and intensely: we were both oddly fatalistic about opportunity and believed, stupidly, that relationships should be easy.

That night we went out for dinner. While he'd hinted at, and I believe had had, a wild few years, now he professed to leading a rather monklike existence. He only worked and walked, he said, and he thought mostly of the stock market, of candlestick charts and valuations and fifty-day moving averages. He said he was a bit depressed about it.

I told him what had happened to me. I'd been working at the comic-book shop for a couple of years, had been trying to make my own comics with limited success, and I, too, was in a bit of a slump.

We sat there at the diner, both looking a little morose, and I wondered if it hadn't after all been a mistake to go out. But then Vu got a funny look on his face.

"What are you thinking?"

"Let's make some comic books together. Like when we were kids."

"Really?"

"Why not? Maybe it could lead to something."

"Do you have something in mind? An idea?"

"Boatloads."

"Like?"

"Superheroes going out to lunch, complaining to their therapists, unsure about their parenting styles. A chase scene where the driver and his passenger, while making split-second decisions, talk about different forms of resistance to power. A murder mystery where the detective receives a call at the crime scene from her father and she tells him her theories about the history of suicide protests around the world, analyses of madness and megalomania versus desperate agency, and the dangers of aestheticizing violence."

"Do you have a name?"

"What do you think? Let's call it *Team Chaos*."

And so Vu and I began making comics together. For some reason, he didn't want to illustrate. He said he'd write but he'd lost interest in drawing. Before, I'd drawn in a more traditional style, but for *Team Chaos* I allowed myself greater freedom. I drew sometimes abstractly or illustrated by collage or sometimes rendered glossy and detailed panoramas. Or, at other times, I drew carefully cross-hatched portraits or photo-realistic cityscapes and apartment rooms.

Our first collaboration worked out one of Vu's ideas, a rather cynical one, I'd thought: A woman who has a nervous breakdown leaves her family. Simultaneously her city erupts in protest against an unfair power structure that guarantees only oppression and inequality. She takes part in the protest, perhaps because, she thinks, the meaninglessness and isolation that led to her breakdown is infused in the systems of economy and ideology the protesters are hoping to dismantle. Or, looming in the back of her mind, maybe she's a coward and this is just another way to run away. She wanders the protesting crowd, tries her hand, on an impulse, at direct action. Immediately she's arrested and put in jail. She's released only years later to find nothing has changed and that she's in the same broken, empty place as before, but now without even the option of protest or escape.

We began publishing our comic on the web, under pseudonym. We call ourselves Ms. Mistleto after the chief villain of Vu's plots. Almost immediately we draw a large and responsive audience.

Mostly we worked together virtually. He'd send me some text, and I'd respond with some sketches. We did this for several years. Occasionally we would get together but less and less over time. After not seeing him in person for weeks, one day Vu texts me to meet him at a bar and that he has something important to tell me.

We sit down at a table, and after ordering our drinks Vu says his father had gotten in touch. His parents divorced long ago, and Vu hadn't heard from his father in years. He says they were never really close.

The father had said he was dying and wanted to see him one last time. At least that's what he seemed to have said. The father gave Vu an address in L.A. and Vu had flown out there. Vu says:

Flying to L.A. from New York is a science fiction novel. You board either in overwhelming swelter or face-burning cold. Either way the sky is gray, the streets are dirty, the air smells of exhaust and sewage. Then the plane obliterates time. You exit this machine some indiscernible era later and walk out onto a tarmac below a cloudless blue sky. The air is dry and temperate and smells faintly of desert flowers. Even the name of the airport is otherworldly: Bob Hope.

It was just before dusk when I'd landed. I drove my rental car on L.A. highways turning coppery under the Martian sun. My father's house was not the one I'd expected. The last address I'd known him to have was a run-down studio on the edge of Echo Park. Where I was heading now was a much more exclusive setting, a white-marble-and-glass lookout nestled into Runyon Canyon.

I was further surprised when my father opened the door. I'd expected the man I'd grown up with, or a more weath-

ered version of him, someone disheveled and angry, someone worn-out but still bright-eyed with unextinguished rage,
a man ready to be disappointed or to lash out. And so I'd
involuntarily taken a deep breath before ringing the door-
bell. I thought he might be reduced by ill health, perhaps
more timid or physically weaker, but I also was convinced
he'd be fundamentally, underneath any bodily metamor-
phosis, unchanged.

He was smiling when he opened the door. The perenni-
ally unfashionable man was well dressed. Crisp, dark blue
pants and a well-cut, pale olive shirt. He gestured me in.

"A lot has happened," he said in an overly friendly manner.

"I can see that. Did you marry an heiress?"

He laughed. "I invented something successful."

"Ah, finally."

"Yes, finally."

I was no longer sure why I'd come. I thought suddenly I
didn't want to have anything to do with him, especially or
particularly if he was happy. At least in a very abstract way,
I was glad for him—but I didn't want anything to do with
it. "You seem healthy," I said.

"Very," he said, and tapped his chest.

"But your message said you were dying."

"I said I didn't have long."

"What does that mean?"

"That I'm going away and I wanted to see you one last
time."

I turned over what he was saying. "That . . . seems selfish. If I understand you correctly."

"I wanted to give you something too."

I nodded. I couldn't think of anything he could give me that I wanted.

He stood up, walked to a desk, and took a book from on top of it. He handed it to me. It was a thin paperback book. It felt new and the binding was tight. Nothing was written on the front of it, but when I opened it I read, on the first page, the words *Dear Cyborgs*.

"What is this?" I asked.

"A program, a drug uploaded through your eyeballs, an idea virus. Technically a bio-based cybernetic machine to collapse space-time, or psychosomatically one that activates clairvoyance, or, more poetically: a time machine. If you read it, you can know the future or the past."

"What?"

"Just kidding. It's my autobiography, kind of. My life story, but fictionalized. I had it printed so I could give it to you. I wanted . . . It doesn't exactly offer excuses, and at this point I'm not sure if my apologies would matter—"

"They wouldn't."

"No, they wouldn't. Not now. But I am sorry."

"Okay. Whatever."

"Well, in any case, this tells my story. As close to the truth as I could make it."

"As close?"

"I made it fiction to tell the truth better, to tell it more fully. It's not exactly the entire truth, but close. Closer than if I tried to tell it straight. I hope it will allow you to learn who I am, who I was."

"I don't understand."

"Here, just take the book. Read it tonight—"

"Tonight?"

"Yes, tonight. Just do me that favor. And we'll talk about it in the morning."

"You want me to read this now?"

"Yes, are you hungry? Do you want something to drink?"

"What? No."

"Okay, here. This is a good chair. And this is a good reading light. I'm going to go out, okay?" He was already putting on his jacket. "You just read that, okay?" He started backing away. "Just do me the favor. It isn't so long. Good night." I heard him go through the hall. I heard the front door open and close, and I heard his car pulling out and driving off. My hesitation had locked me onto a path. It would've been easy enough to refuse him, to have cursed him and just walked out. Or even after he'd left, I could have simply put the book down, got in my car, and joined the glowing bugs of the L.A. freeways. But I didn't. I sat there. And after a moment I picked up the book. I started reading.

It was short, and it really only took me a few hours to read. I finished the last page and stood up to stretch. An odd story, it was composed of many shorter, similar stories. If it was a confessional novel it was also a puzzle with a fractal structure, and it mutated and yet duplicated its shape by my changing focus and perspective on it.

I could guess at his apology and I perhaps better

understood his rage, but my sympathy for my father had a hard limit.

I yawned. I was tired and figured in any case that I should get some sleep. I'd confront him with my questions in the morning. Reading the book had felt significant, but I didn't yet understand how much it had changed me. I found a blanket and fell asleep on the couch.

That night I had a dream.

In my dream I see my father. He is saying goodbye to me just as he'd done the previous day. I see him put on his jacket and go out his front door, leaving me to read his book.

He gets in his car and drives off. He is crying but then he composes himself. He drives to the airport. He has a plane ticket and, already packed in the car, a small suitcase. I watch him catch a flight to Fairbanks, Alaska.

On the plane he takes a napkin and writes on it: "I'm sorry. Goodbye," and then, after a moment, "I love you."

He takes his time finishing his drink. And when he is finished he crumples up the napkin, puts it in his empty plastic cup, and passes it to the flight attendant, who is coming down the aisle to collect trash.

When my father arrives in Fairbanks, he buys a bottle of whiskey and rents a car. He drives to a remote cabin three hours away. Then, that night, when the temperature falls to thirty below, he takes the bottle and walks out into the wintery air.

Just a few feet from his cabin he suddenly takes off his coat and drops it to the ground. Soon he begins trembling all over. Gulping slugs of whiskey cannot prevent his hands from shaking. He keeps walking.

He doesn't seem to have a particular destination and just heads north through a sparse wood. It's a clear night and the moon drapes the unbroken carpet of snow. There are no animal noises and only the occasional breeze through the boughs. His face is grim and set and his steps begin to become uneven, staggering. After an hour or so he collapses. He then closes his eyes and, after some time, he dies.

I wake up and know my dream is true. I thought this is just my father's typical type of perversion: to commit suicide in this way and force me to bear witness. It made me furious.

The next day I fly back to New York. A couple of weeks later I'm not at all surprised when I receive a call from the Alaskan police notifying me that a body has been found. I refuse to identify my father, and he is buried in a pauper's grave.

I start noting the changes over the next month. First only isolated episodes but then a flurry that merged with current time until I thought I was going insane. I'd pick up the newspaper and read a profile of the newly elected mayor but then would be confused because, later in the week, I'd hear, on live TV, the voting results come in. I'd walk down the street and see a car accident. It would happen right in front of me, but then I'd blink and all evidence of it would be gone, as if the camera angle hadn't changed but a sudden jump cut had removed all the evidence from the scene.

My stock charts would project forward, and I was at first overjoyed but then frightened, because making vast sums suddenly became trivial. I passed a storefront and saw raging fire, which disappeared when I shook my head—but then this same building was ashes a few days later.

"Listen," Vu says, "you see the future but it's helpless. It's all incredible, fantastic—at first. Then it turns horrible. Clairvoyance. Maybe there's a way out. Maybe it's not hopeless, not impossible. I'm giving this to you. It's a curse but maybe it's also a shot. I'm sorry. Read it. You'll understand." And then Vu got up and left.

I was in shock so didn't stop him. When I came to, so to speak, he was gone and I was left staring at the book on the restaurant table. I took it and went home.

The next few days I kept calling and texting Vu, but he didn't respond. I grew worried and finally went over to his apartment. The super let me in. The place was cleaned out. Vu had left without a trace.

I went back home and stared at his book. I knew Vu wanted me to read it, that perhaps he'd left some message or explanation there, but I couldn't bring myself to do it. I didn't believe in Vu's story, at least I didn't think I did, but I'd been spooked by it.

I put the book in a box and put the box underneath my bed.

Years passed.

These, for me, weren't good years. I kept losing jobs. I drank too much. I spent a great many evenings talking to Vu. I'd take the book out of the box and put it on my kitchen table. "Hi, Vu," I'd say. "Where the fuck did you go?" and "I miss you" and "My life is a mess." But I still couldn't bring myself to read the book, and the knowledge of my cowardice made me drink even more.

One evening coming home from a job I hated and was on the verge of getting fired from, I came across a chanting crowd at Zuccotti Park. I took a second to listen and bothered to read a pamphlet that someone shoved into my hands, but I was about to move on when I saw a familiar face, one I hadn't seen in a long time.

I walked over and tapped a woman on the shoulder. "Are you, is, is that, are you Frank's sister?"

She turned around, startled, and then looked at my face. I saw a smile of recognition and she said my name. "Oh my god. It's been a long time."

"Years."

We went off to get a drink.

"So whatever happened," she asked, after we'd been talking for an hour, "to Vu? You and he were making those sick comics together."

"You liked them?"

"They were great. I was in on a great secret, it felt. And then you seemed to disappear."

"Yeah."

"You just stopped. Mid-story. That felt right too, even if it left me bereft. Some tragedy or act of integrity seemed behind it but unexplained. Just radio silence."

"Not integrity. Tragedy.'

"What happened?"

"I don't know," I said. And so, after a moment, I told her about my last conversation with Vu.

I could see her fascination grow. I was drunk by then, and I knew I was slurring my words, but I couldn't stop either drinking or talking. On the other hand, she'd stopped drinking and was looking more and more intense.

"You haven't seen him since?"

"No."

After a moment she said, "You have to show me the book."

"Okay," I said weakly.

"No—now," she said.

"What, now?"

"Now."

And while I knew this was the one important secret around which I'd built my recent life, there occurred to me the craven, simple idea that this woman wanted to come home with me.

———

In the cab there, which she paid for, she said, "The problem is that history is not a dialectic progression but a biome, a swamp where ideas chase each other around and wallow and where drupelets of their larvae cluster and then hatch to devour siblings."

"What?" I said.

"I tried shoplifting and arson at first, then participation in electoral politics both at the local and state level. I contemplated car theft and assassination. Social work and immigration law. At night I think about the Unabomber or buying large tracts of Midwestern land. None of it makes sense."

I shook my head. "What?" I asked again.

"When we were kids my brother and I were alone," she said. "No one else would play with us. Maybe because we were immigrants, I'm not sure. Or maybe because we were twins and so formed a clique others felt was impenetrable. In any case we played alone most of the time, just us two. Our games were always competitions. Games of wit or logic or strength but with a clear winner and loser. Staring matches, chicken, bike races, arm wrestling. It didn't matter he was a boy and I was a girl. One game we played a lot was who could hold on to the monkey bars the longest. Frank would narrate. We'd get in position, hanging there, and he would describe the stakes. He said we were hanging for our lives. Below us was a portal to a hell into which the first to let go would fall forever and where demons would bite out your eyes and spear you in the gut and through your arms and legs and genitals throughout your infinite plunge. My brother detailed it. And I believed him. The second to let go, he said, was the winner. And that person would land on the grass *in this mundane world*, he always called it. I believed him. I remember laughing with him at first, hanging from the monkey bars, goading him, saying, 'You're gonna fall! You're weak!' and then feeling the pain creep up my arms to my fingers, which I knew were weakening, were slipping, and burning burning with the approaching limit.

"I fell first," she went on, "or I fell second, but whenever we played, even though it was a favorite, important game for us, maybe because of this, I always cried. Not then. Not in front of him. Later. At night, under covers, or in my secret hiding spot in the basement closet. I'd cry either out of grief for him or shame at myself."

We got to my apartment. She sat at my kitchen table, no longer talking, no longer animated, just, it seemed obvious to me, waiting.

I resigned myself to disaster and went to the bedroom and brought out Vu's book from its place in the box underneath my bed. I'd never even opened it. But as soon as I put it on the table in front of her, she opened the book and began reading.

"Do you want another drink?" I asked, but she just shook her head. I made myself one and went into the other room and sat on the couch thinking she'd join me there. But she didn't come. She just kept reading at the table.

In the end I fell asleep on the couch.

And then, hours later, in the morning she woke me up and had a strangely focused and determined look on her face. And when I asked what was going on, she confirmed something I had, somewhere deep down, already long known—that Vu was dead. But before that, in the moments when I was sitting and waiting for her on the couch, I was struck by an odd combination of exhaustion and excitement. I was exhausted from work and from the long night of drinking, but I was simultaneously also terrified and excited by what she might reveal.

Maybe Vu had left detailed instructions, a plan, a rendezvous, a map, a strategy for final revenge. I kept nodding off. It was a terrible waiting. The more I fought to stay awake, the more I flashed through dreams and nightmares and visions that must have lasted only seconds but felt like intense weeks or impressionistic lifetimes. Eventually I fell asleep, but over that half hour as I fought it, I ran through various chase scenes, loved and had bitter fights, mourned future and past dead, cursed and was cursed, tried grandiose heists only to be caught and jailed and tortured and then set free, went hungry, ate elegant meals at long tables, mourned and was chased and chased and fought and mourned and mourned and mourned and mourned.

Acknowledgments

Thanks to the editors of the following publications, where portions of this novel appeared in slightly different form: *The Coming Envelope*, *Dazed*, *Your Impossible Voice*, and *Vestiges*. For the gifts of sass and hope provided in uneven proportions, I'm grateful to the outstanding students who are found in the Hunter College High School Library. My profound thanks also to: Donald Breckenridge, Lisa Chen, Lynn Crawford, Alan Davies, Corey Frost, Jeremy Hoevenaar, Ellen Israel, John Knight, Ning Li, Kun Boo and Keun Hee and Karen Lim, Alex Samsky, Lisa Siegmann, Marya Spence, Shannon Steneck, Jamil Thomas, Cassie and Danny Tunick, John Yau, and Leni Zumas.

For Joanna, my first reader, and for Felix, our son who cannot yet read, my gratitude goes beyond words.

31901067381105